"After reading the story of Cliff and Serena I was very touched by their love and devotion to each other. Their story is one that everyone wishes to find in their life. The characters were believable with just a hint of supernatural to make this book shine. I look forward to many more books from this author."

Carrie M, from Lafayette, LA

"I loved this book, it is an easy read, suspenseful and romantic. The fact that it is locally staged makes you feel like you are right there with them. Can't wait for the next one."

Giselle S, from Salem, OR

"Good story, lovable character and a nice twist on the paranormal romance."

Destiny T, from Salem, OR

"Good story, I can see the characters clearly in my mind and put them is the scenes painted in the book. There is a nice twist to the story and a wicked cliffhanger ending."

Dave O, from Stayton, OR

"Love *Heart and Souls*, characters are inviting and easy to relate to. I was pulled into Serena's world from the beginning and felt her emotional highs and lows right along with her. Hard to put down and can't wait until the next one."

Lisa S, from Salem, OR

"The storyline captured that whimsical place in my heart. I couldn't put it down. Serena is captivating and down to earth and I love her personality, sizzling romance with Cliff. I felt like part of the story and could see myself being a customer in her coffee shop.

"The mystery of James is one I wanted to unravel with Serena, I felt like I was uncovering all the clues right alongside her. Loved how their lives intertwined."

Heather H, from San Diego, CA

The Spirit of Love: Heart and Souls

Linda K. Richison

This is a work of fiction.
Names, characters, organizations, places, events, and incidents are either products or the author's imagination or are used fictitiously.

Copyright © 2016 Linda K. Richison

ISBN: 1511458704
ISBN-13: 978-1511458702

Printed in the United States of America

DEDICATIONS

During the writing of this book I was blessed to have had the support and encouragement from my loving family and friends that are dear to my heart. I wish I could list everyone, as you all played a big part in making this book a success, but I can't fit you all in this limited space.

There are a few special people that have followed along with my entire journey that I would like to recognize. First, I would like to thank God for giving me this gift to write and opening my heart and eyes to see it. For my husband Ron that supported me with my crazy idea of writing a book. My sister and best friend Carrie Ann Morrisette, that believed in my dream and offered her creativity and expertise. Giselle Strauch, my good neighbor and friend which read my book with excitement and enthusiasm, always eager to read the next chapter. My dear friend, Lisa Strom for all the grueling hours she spent reading and re-reading and editing the chapters and offering her ideas. Crystal LaFrance my sister-in-law and Heather Crain my future daughter-in-law, for their love and desire for reading and their on-going support.

Of course, I never would've been able to get started and work towards publication if it hadn't been for my consultant; Annette Trucke a very sweet lady that helped me define a plan, JoAnn Kempfer who took my idea and with her magic fingers, produced the first draft of my book cover and Rick Southerland, graphic artist extraordinaire; who formatted the chapters of my book, designed the cover and prepared them for print. It takes a collaboration of many people, all with special talents to make a book a success I was blessed to have had the best.

Last but not least my dogs that were not at all pleased with me when I spent hours at the computer writing instead of playing with them. The walk hasn't always been easy on this journey but each and every one of you kept me going and I will be forever grateful.

TO MY READERS

Thank you for choosing my book, and I'd like to welcome you to "The Spirit of Love" series. I hope you enjoy them as much as I did writing them.

I created the characters to entertain you with their witty humor, romantic interludes and a touch of mystical fantasy. They are sure to make their way into your heart and come alive in your mind as they take you on an exciting journey of adventure and mystery.

So please enjoy the peek into the books of "The Spirit of Love" series below:

Heart and Souls

> Serena put the book down and stepped back. "Oh no, that is never going to happen, Serena said, slowly backing away from it as if it were a live reptile. "I am not helping you or any other trapped soul. My life is just starting to get back on track and helping you was not on the list of getting there. I am truly sorry but I just can't go there right now."

"Serena," the voice coming from the book, pleaded. "Please, you have to help me. I need to know who I am, how I got here and how to get free. I beg of you."

Lost and Found

The man, still trying to hold his ground commented, "It's probably nothing more than a virtual image she created to scare people off. But it's not going to scare me." But after James lowered himself close to the man's level and circle around the team a few times, Serena could tell the man didn't believe that to be true.

Serena stood facing the couple, pepper spray aimed directly at them, strongly stated. "Now get out of my store and don't you ever come back or I will show you what the spirit can really do. I believe there was an order signed by the Judge that clearly stated you were not allowed anywhere near this store or me. I was fortunate to get a picture of you two and I am not afraid to show it to the police. Now go!!!" Serena yelled out moving the spray closer to them.

Serena's plan had worked, the couple wasted no time in vacating her store. She laughed as she watched them scurry away like two defeated rats.

Matt, now getting a little irritated by the game, called out. "Ok what or whoever you are come out and show yourself."

Of course, the fairy (Lily) had a stubborn streak and was not about to be ordered around by some stranger. So peaking around the corner she abruptly answered. "No one orders me around, I will appear when I am ready and not before."

Great, Matt thought, not only do I have a fairy occupying my home; she has a snippety attitude. He had to find a way to get her out of his house. The problem was he didn't have a clue how he was supposed to do that.

CONTENTS

"Life is not measured by the breaths you take, but the moments that take your breath away."

Maya Angelou

1) BREAKING UP

It was April 24th 2015 at seven o'clock on a dreary Saturday morning, which Serena thought was way too early for her to be having a serious conversation with Kevin, her fiancé. She had been awakened by a knock at her door 30 minutes ago and was surprised to see him standing there, especially after he had canceled their dinner plans the night before to attend a last minute business meeting. He said there was something important he needed to talk to her about and it couldn't wait until later.

Serena sat curled up on the sofa peering at Kevin through her matted fiery red hair. She was pretty sure her brain was still in bed because she was having a difficult time concentrating on what he was saying to her. He also didn't seem quite like himself, but Serena couldn't put her finger on it. Unknown to her, he was about to destroy their perfect little world.

Serena wasn't sure who was currently possessing her 6'1" wavy brown haired, green-eyed handsome fiancé's body. It looked like him, but this man standing in her living room had a distant faraway look in his eyes. "What did you do with my fiancé?" Serena asked with a look of confusion on her face. "What's going on here Kevin? You are starting to scare me with all this talk about how we don't fit

1

together anymore?"

"Serena," said Kevin seriously, pleading his defense. "I don't want to hurt you. It's just that we want different things in life. I'm not sure we are right for one another. There was a time I felt that to be true, but these last few months I've been doing a lot of thinking and decided I'm not ready for a lifetime commitment." Kevin paused and took a deep breath before completing his thought. He knew it wasn't going to be easy for Serena to accept, but it needed to be said. "In fact, I think we need some time apart to make sure this is what we really want."

Serena's face froze while she tried to comprehend what was happening. Just last week she had been picking out her wedding invitations and making plans for the big day, and now it seemed like all that was vanishing. She felt like she had ventured into the twilight zone. She brushed a strand of hair out of her eyes so she could see Kevin more clearly and then carefully replied, "I know in my heart this is what I want. I don't need any time apart!" With a deep sigh, Serena continued. "Why all of a sudden are you having a change of heart? Kevin, maybe you are just getting cold feet. I have heard that this sometimes happens to people before they get married. I am kind of lost here; you were the one who said we belonged together and that we were soul mates. I thought you were happy; we were happy," Serena said, watching her fiancé, not too sure her bruised emotions could survive his answer.

Out of habit, Kevin put his hands in his pockets and looked away. "I realized I wasn't really happy, just content. I need to travel, experience new things, go out more, take up dancing or try skydiving. You seem to be content working all the time, and on your days off you are either lazing around or taking care of mundane tasks. We are driving a Suburban and at our age, we should be driving a Ferrari."

Serena cringed. Her brain definitely wasn't firing on all cylinders because Kevin didn't seem to be making much sense to her. Where was he coming up with these crazy ideas? They did a lot of things together. Trying to stay in the conversation, Serena stated. "Kevin, we don't own a Suburban. Would you like a Ferrari? We can look into getting one if that is what you want. If you want to do all those things I am open to listening. You know we have always worked things out in the past." With her head pounding, she asked. "Can we please have some coffee and discuss this rationally?"

Kevin let out a big sigh and shook his head. "Not this time Serena, this is something that can't be resolved over a cup of coffee. It needs to be dealt with here and now so we both can move on with our lives. You seem to be missing the point. I don't want a Ferrari! I just used that as a metaphor to describe how I view our lives," Kevin replied.

Serena thought to herself. I still want a cup of coffee! She needed something tangible to hold on to, and the caffeine might steady her shaking hands and clear the cobwebs in her head.

"Serena you don't understand, I don't want this, us, anymore! I need to figure out what I really want. I need some space and time," Kevin replied in frustration.

Serena still wasn't quite sure where this was going. A sick feeling started forming in her stomach, as she realized her Cinderella story may be falling apart... she was losing her prince. Reality was sinking in. Kevin was really leaving her. This seemed so surreal to Serena, things like this only happened in books and movies, not in her life.

Silent tears cascaded down Serena's cheeks as his empty eyes stared back at her. What had just happened? Serena wanted to talk; to express what she was thinking, but her thoughts and words were jumbled in her head and she couldn't make any sense out of them.

This strange man, who used to be her best friend, sat down next to her. She knew he was talking but she couldn't hear him over the headache that had taken up residence in her head. She heard only bits and pieces of what was being said. What did register was; that she worked too much, never had time for him, didn't like to go out and... Serena shut him out as he droned on and on explaining all his false reasons. She abruptly pulled herself back to the present when he mentioned someone named Tanya. From what Serena could gather they had been working closely on an assignment, and he may have developed feelings for her.

It was all sinking in now and Serena was finally getting a clear picture of what was happening. She hoped this was a bad dream and any minute she would wake up, and things would be back to normal between Kevin and her. But she knew that wasn't a possibility. He had found someone else and was leaving her. His talk about needing time was an excuse, just a lie. Serena wondered how long she had been living in this lie.

She had heard somewhere that when trauma hits, you go through phases; Shock (been there!), Denial (done that), Hurt (totally there) Anger, then Acceptance. Serena was definitely moving past the hurt stage, plummeting swiftly into anger with full force while acceptance was inconceivable

A broken Serena, now fully awake and riding on an emotional adrenaline high, rose up off the couch and stood in front of Kevin. With her body tense and fist clenched, she took her stance as she faced him. "Your acting is perfectly staged, but you don't fool me. It's all lies. You have no right blaming our relationship faults on me, how dare you sit there and make all these false accusations about me, when you have been cheating on me for who knows how long?" Serena cried, raising her arms above her head in frustration. "I am not going to take the blame for the dissolution of our relationship." Serena stated in her defense.

Serena looked away and tried to be strong but the hurt and the anger left her vulnerable. She was having a difficult time controlling her emotions and the streams of tears falling down her cheeks. She folded her arms hoping to stop her body from trembling. With darts of anger in her eyes, Serena continued. "How could you let me believe that we were going to build a life together? I gave you my heart and was about to become your wife. You said meeting me was the best thing that ever happened to you. I can see now that those were just worthless words. I have wasted a lot of time and invested so much in this relationship, not to mention the time and money that went into preparing for a wedding that isn't going to happen. How could you just throw us away just like that?" Serena said, reaching for a tissue.

Kevin stood up and stared at Serena in bewilderment. He hadn't imagined the news would hit her this hard. Obviously, he had been wrong. He still cared for her; he just didn't want to be with her anymore. He was in love with someone else and someday she would understand. He had to be careful in choosing his next words. Given the fragile state she was in, he didn't want to cause her any more pain. "Serena, please, believe me, I never meant for this to happen. It just did and it's not fair to live here with you when my heart is somewhere else. I know that there is a special someone out there for you and I hope you find him. Believe it or not Serena, I do want the best for you and you deserve to find happiness."

Kevin's words cut Serena like a knife. If he didn't want to hurt her why was he doing this? What did Tanya have that she didn't? She felt so alone and lost. Part of her wanted to forgive him; beg and plead for him to stay. She longed to feel his loving arms around her and his lips pressing gently against hers. But a bigger part, the one filled with disgust knowing those arms and lips had touched another, simply wanted him as far away as possible.

Serena placed her face in her hands and lightly shook her head, hoping this brief pause would allow her to find some control. She was tired, her body was numb and she just wanted to be alone. Serena looked up and stared at Kevin, who was leaning against the chair with hands in his pocket and his head down. "Kevin, I think you should leave now. I have nothing more to say to you. Serena walked to the front door and opened it. With her right arm she motioned for him to leave. "Get out of my house, go drive your Ferrari with Tanya." ('Over a cliff'), a quiet thought bubble formed in her head. With that, Kevin silently headed for the door and before leaving, he turned around and said to Serena, "I am truly sorry."

Serena watched him walk out the door and out of her life like a billow of lingering smoke. "NO, YOU'RE NOT!" she screamed, picking up a vase and throwing it at the door that closed quickly behind him. She watched as the remnants scattered to the floor, like pieces breaking inside her heart.

Serena's body trembled as she thought to herself, what was she going to do now? What would her life look like? Leaning against the foyer wall she slid down holding her knees in a crouched position. She cried softly and remained frozen in that position until she could find the strength to make her way to the couch. Empty and emotionally drained, she curled up into a ball. Wrapping her arms tightly around a throw pillow, she gradually let sleep shelter her from the pain.

By early afternoon, Serena jumped awake at the sound of her cell phone. Through her blurry eyes she saw her Dad's number. Serena knew she should pick it up but she didn't want to talk to anyone now. He would hear the pain in her voice and want an explanation and she wasn't even sure what had happened. Besides, her head still hurt and all she wanted to do was feel sorry for herself and sleep. It was her day off and she intended on having a pity party. Didn't she deserve it? Serena ignored the phone and fell back to sleep.

Three hours later Serena awoke with her head still pounding. She needed food, coffee and something to dull the ache in her head. The thought of food made her gag, but maybe toast would quiet her rumbling stomach and ease the headache a bit.

She went into the bathroom for some aspirin and saw her reflection in the mirror. She sure wasn't going to win any beauty contests today, not unless bloodshot eyes and matted wild hair was on the list of qualifications. Serena just didn't care. She was taking this pity party seriously.

After forcing down a piece of toast, gagging on a couple aspirin and pushing two cups of coffee into her body, Serena's cell phone rang again. Tess, her sister was calling. First her dad and now her sister, she probably should see if something was wrong. Serena couldn't take anymore today. If one more thing happened she'd need to switch to something much stronger than coffee.

"Hey Sis, what's happening?" Tess asked, with an ever-loving positive lift in her voice.

"Not much. It's my day off and I'm just feeling a bit lazy today," Serena replied, hoping to keep the sadness out of her voice.

"Are you sure everything is ok? You sound sad."

Busted! Tess could always tell when something wasn't right. Call it a sixth sense or maybe intuition. "Never could hide anything from you, Sis. Well, if you must know, Kevin and I had a talk this morning and he decided to leave me, but I really don't want to discuss it now. Why don't you come over tonight, bring some wine and your pajamas, we'll spend the night drinking, talking and I can cry on your shoulder."

What do you mean, 'decided to leave'?" her sister asked in a confused voice. This had come as a total shock to Tess, who was going to be the Maid of Honor in Serena's wedding in a few months. Maybe they had a fight and he left for a while. Hopefully, that was the case.

"Tess, can we please talk about this later? I really don't want to go into it over the phone," Serena said, pleading with her sister.

Tess knowing she wasn't going to find out any answers now, decided to let it go. "Okay, I understand and won't press it. I am just worried about you especially when you sound so upset. Anyway, I'll check with Tom and see if he will watch the girls tonight. I'm sure it won't be a problem so if I don't call you back then it's a go. I could really use a night away! It's been awhile since we've had a girl's night," Tess replied, still a little shocked by the news. She also wondered what Serena and Kevin had talked about, and the meaning behind her sister's statement "he decided to leave me." It must be pretty serious for her to want a wine-laced get-together. Normally her sister was the upbeat happy one and was consoling her. Hopefully, she would be able to talk with her tonight to find out the details.

"How are Tom and the girls?" Serena asked, wanting to change the subject.

"You know Tom, always has a project going. I think I married Tim the tool man, and your nieces; they challenge their boundaries every day. Between them and the puppy, Chaos, there is never a dull moment at our house," Tess said with a laugh.

Tess was married to a wonderful man who had blessed her with two beautiful daughters; Crissy, who was seven and Stephanie, who was nine. Serena adored the girls and loved spoiling them every chance she could. Serena also loved her brother-in-law, he was just like the brother she never had. Tom was a good husband and father. She was so happy for her sister.

"Hey Serena!" said Tess, "I almost forgot the reason I called. Dad called and said he couldn't get a hold of you and asked if I knew where you were." I told him you were probably busy but I would check to make sure everything was okay, and I am sure glad I did."

"Anyway," Tess continued. "Dad got a call from our cousin Lucy. You know, Aunt Caroline's daughter. As you may recall, Caroline left Lucy the bookstore in her will. Well, Lucy doesn't want the store; it's hard for her to juggle raising a family and running a business full time. So guess what, lucky sister? You are the next person noted in the will to get the store. Congratulations, you are the proud owner of 'Books on the Corner' in Astoria!"

Serena couldn't believe what Tess was telling her. In reaction to the shocking news, she almost landed on the floor while attempting to sit down on the couch. Could this day get any stranger? What in the world was she going to do with a bookstore? She was already the CEO of their dad's coffee business and managed ten coffee shops in the Portland area; that kept her more than busy enough. They were currently looking for a new location for another coffee shop but not at the coast. It was too far away. Was God playing a trick on her? It certainly wasn't funny. She had lost her fiancé and gained a bookstore all in the same day! What were the odds?

"Tess," Serena said, trying to get her balance back from her near fall. "Are you sure that I own the bookstore? Is it possible someone made a mistake?" Serena asked hopefully.

"You'll need to call Dad and get all the details. I'm just the messenger," Tess replied.

"Hey, Serena, I need to go take care of the girls and talk with Tom about tonight. We can talk more about it later when we get our sisters on! Love ya," Tess lovingly stated.

"Love you too! And sis, don't worry. I will be okay," Serena answered, wondering if she sounded any more convincing to her sister than she did to herself.

Serena couldn't wait to talk with Tess. It would be nice to have someone with her tonight, and now she had a guest for her pity party.

After getting off the phone with Tess, she returned her dad's call, only to be greeted by a short voicemail. She left him a message that she would call him tomorrow, said I love you and ended the call.

2) PICKING UP THE PIECES

Serena stared blankly at her surroundings. She could feel Kevin's presence everywhere. From the coffee cup he left on the side table earlier that morning, to the pictures on the wall of the two of them, so happy, at a friend's wedding last year. It might be time to think about moving. She wondered if she could erase the memories as easily as finding a new location. Moving wouldn't be so hard, she thought. Her living room held the standard couch, a coffee table with a few minor scratches, nothing that couldn't be recovered with a good oil finish; it was comfortable, clean and neat. A couple of abstract pieces of art she had picked up at a bazaar that blended well with her personality were displayed on the wall. The corner wall was just large enough to hold her fifty-five inch flat screen television. The kitchen, open and overlooking the living room, held the normal appliances and there was a small table off to the side that fit four comfortably. Nearby, next to the kitchen, her stacked compact washer and dryer fit snug in an enclosed closet. There was one bath in her apartment adjacent to the master bedroom. Her bedroom was her favorite room on which she had lavished extra attention. In that room she had spent more money on the furniture and bedding, which included a beautiful rose duvet that adorned her mahogany canopy bed. A matching full dresser and chest of drawers sat on adjacent walls. A small closet, customized to suit her needs still barely accommodated all of her clothes. It wasn't much, but she was happy here. It was her home.

Serena had for the past several years, been putting aside money for the down payment on her dream home. The home she envisioned her and Kevin sharing for years to come. Now she was left with a painful ache in her heart and empty lonely dreams.

Of course with all that was going on at the moment, now was not the time to be reflecting back; there would be plenty of time for that. Right now she needed to shower and pick up a little bit. Tess would be arriving in a couple of hours and now she had a broken vase to add to the clean-up list. Even though the thought of food still nauseated her, Serena knew that it was imperative that they didn't drink on an empty stomach. She opted for pizza, since she didn't feel like cooking. It was one of her favorite comfort foods and would pair perfectly with her Zinfandel. She only hoped she would feel like eating by the time the pizza arrived.

Serena made her best attempt to clean up her little apartment. Right now even the littlest tasks were a challenge for her weary soul. She tried to keep focused but memories of her and Kevin plague her mind. She felt a certain disconnection with her surroundings, like a stranded dog lost on a deserted highway. Her life had no sense of direction and it didn't help that she was in a flux of internal confusion. She was still struggling with the thought of her and Kevin living separate lives, and the irony of it all, she was contemplating giving him another chance if he came back.

All she wanted to do was drown in her tears of sorrow and then fall into a deep sleep to escape from the pain. After going through the motions to make her home presentable, Serena dragged her tired body, under protest, into the bathroom for a quick shower. She hoped that it might temporarily wash away Kevin's ghostly touches on her skin while she longed for the real thing.

After her shower, Serena tied her mass of thick, rich tresses of dark red hair on top of her head. She stared at her reflection in the mirror and a wounded soul glared back at her. Her eyes were red and very puffy due to a morning of crying and undue stress. Damn that man! Look at me! I am a wreck, she thought. Luckily she had some eye drops and Prep H, a must have for the late-night-early-morning-after eye puffiness. Serena reached for the tube but accidently grabbed the tube of sore muscle cream instead. Kevin had left it there when he had injured his shoulder last year. Her mind was elsewhere and she didn't notice her mistake. Upon putting it on, her doorbell rang. Serena turned too quickly and accidently touched her finger to her eye and it immediately started burning. With blurry eyes, she caught sight of the tube. "Oh shit!" She gasped. Her doorbell rang again and Serena yelled, "Be there in just a minute!" She splashed some cold water in her eye to help soothe the burning, covered herself with her favorite purple robe and went to the door.

Serena was met at the door by a young sandy-haired delivery boy with blue eyes. At the sight of her disheveled form, his eyes grew as big as saucers. The young boy was standing there holding her pizza with a strange look on his face. He probably thought that she was winking at him because her right eye kept twitching. Politely he told her it was twelve dollars and tried hard not to stare while Serena dug through her purse for her money. She paid for the pizza and included a hefty tip. He certainly deserved it. The poor boy was probably going to have nightmares of the strange lady with red eyes in the purple robe. He took the money, said thank you and hurried back to his truck.

Serena went back up to her apartment and replaced her robe she was wearing with a pair of sweat pants and a t-shirt. She wanted to be comfy. She had flushed out most of the medicine in her eye and was starting to feel a little better. However, she had made both eyes look a little more dramatic with the right one being entirely red-rimmed. She was definitely a sight, she sighed, knowing that her sister would love her anyway.

Tess showed up minutes after Serena's encounter with the pizza boy. She had a loving smile beaming on her face and a bottle of White Zinfandel in her hand. She was dressed in yoga pants, an off-the-shoulder t-shirt and a light jacket. Serena loved her sister but had always been a little envious of her. Standing at 5'5" Tess had a petite athletic body, golden blond hair which she had pulled back in a French braid, and beautiful deep sea-blue eyes that lit up her face. On the other hand, Serena was 5'7", had long, curly, fiery red hair and forest-green eyes. She had never ending legs and the rest of her body was proportioned to her height, even though like many woman, she was always fighting with an unwanted five to seven pounds.

The two had always been close, even though they seemed to be totally different. While Tess was leading the cheers at the football games in high school, Serena was performing in the marching band. While Serena was attending business college, Tess was going to night school to get her beautician license. Tess shopped at Macy's while Serena was happy shopping at Wal-Mart, unless she was looking for professional work attire, then she would splurged at the more higher-end stores. No matter their differences, they were still best friends.

After the meet and greet was over, the two sisters settled in the living room, each with a slice of pizza and a glass of white wine.

"The family sends their love, and here the girls made you something special to help you feel better." Tess said, handing Serena an envelope. Serena was touched by the card the girls had made for her. On the outside were the words, "Be Happy" and on the inside there was a paper folded in half with cut out magazine pictures of birds, butterflies and rainbows glued randomly to the paper. They had printed their first names and finished with, "We love you Aunt Sena." "Sena" was a nickname Stephanie had given her aunt when she was almost two. Serena was touched as she thought about her sweet nieces. She loved Crissy and Stephanie so much, though she admitted to having a softer spot for Crissy, maybe it was because she was the younger one. Brushing away a few escaped tear drops, she put their card on the mantel and sat down on the sofa.

"Also," Tess continued, as she took a seat next to Serena on the sofa,   "Tom said he would kick some sense into that boy for leaving the best thing he ever had; you just say the word."

Serena took a sip of wine as she gave an unrealistic thought to Tom's offer. "As much as that does sound appealing, and he does deserve it, Tom probably wouldn't play the inmate role well or rock the jailhouse attire at all. But I will put it down as an option if the need arises."

Tess giggled at her Serena's statement and put her legs under her to get comfortable. She was eager to hear what her sister and Kevin had talked about that morning. "Well are you going to tell me what happened? You left me in suspense all afternoon. So spill it sister, I want all the details and don't leave anything out!"

So Serena, in between small bites of pizza, many sips of wine and bouts of uncontrollable sobbing, recounted the morning from hell. After all was said and done, Serena thought to herself maybe she should consider Tom's offer. It sounded much more appealing as the alcohol relaxed her, but she quickly pushed the thought out of her mind. She would just let Karma find him. After more hugs, tears, and wine, Serena pulled herself together, and tried to endure the rest of the evening.

She gazed at her sister through her drowsy intoxicated eyes

and said, "Hey, Tess, would you say I am more like a Suburban or a Ferrari?"

Tess pondered that bizarre question a minute before answering. "Neither, I think your style is more like a hybrid... very economical, environmentally safe and decently priced."

"Is that bad?" Serena asked as she tried to sit her slouching body upright. "It does sound kind of boring, sedate," Serena admitted. "Maybe Kevin was right. Here I am almost 30 and what does my life look like?" Serena pondered that question and continued, "I haven't traveled much, and I have no sense of adventure; like bungee jumping or skydiving. Tess, do you realize, I have never even skied?"

Serena leaned her head back against the sofa and closed her tired eyes "I am so pathetic," she whined. Somewhere in the back of her numb mind, Serena knew that it had to be the wine talking because her sober self would never allow her to dream of attempting those acts of craziness. She threw her hands up in the air, then grabbed her head and cried, "I don't want to be just a hybrid!"

Tess stared at her sister who obviously was having a little mental breakdown. Due probably to the morning revelations and maybe helped along by the alcohol she had consumed. Attempting to calm her sister before another bout of tears ensued, she spoke quietly and softly, "Serena, Kevin was not right and don't you ever say that again. You are still very young and have plenty of time to travel and explore crazy adventures. Let's set the bucket list aside for the time being and focus on what you can do to heal yourself."

Curling up on the end of the sofa, Serena rested her head. As she was drifting off to sleep, through her hazy mind, Serena tried to concentrate on what her sister was saying,

"Hey I've got an idea! Let's go to Astoria and check out your bookstore next weekend. Maybe that will help you get your mind off Kevin and who knows, it could be just what you need." Tess stated, looking forward to getting away and a little curious to check out the bookstore.

Serena murmured in a sleepy voice, unaware what she was agreeing to. "Sure sis," then she slipped into a relaxed wine induced sleep.

Tess gently covered her sister with the plush blanket draped over the back of the sofa. She placed a kiss on her cheek, went to get her phone to check in at home, and then find a place to crash. She was feeling okay but she was pretty sure her sister wouldn't be in the morning. The crying, wine and sleeping on the couch were certain to ensure pain. Oh well, thought Tess, no use letting that big bed go to waste.

Serena awoke on the couch the next morning, a little groggy and disoriented. The headache was back again, this time it brought a band with it and it felt like a drum solo was banging inside her head.

Gently she arose to find that her dear sweet sister had left her a glass of water and two aspirins beside a handwritten note on the coffee table. Tess wrote:

Loved the girl time last night, had to get home to get the girls off to school and see Tom before he leaves for work. I also have a full schedule at the salon today. Take the aspirin, try eating some toast and there should be some fresh brewed coffee. I set the timer for nine. I called Nina (Serena's head assistant and good friend) and told her you had a rough day yesterday and you would be in late. I didn't go into details; I figured that's your story to tell. Call me later when you can. Loves and looking forward to our road trip this weekend.

Serena remembered her sister talking about going to Astoria, but didn't remember agreeing to the idea. It must have been the wine doing the talking for her. Maybe it would do her good; she couldn't sit around the apartment all weekend with Kevin's presence following her from room to room, like a cloak of despair.

Serena lied back down on the couch. Memories of the day before flooded her mind. Could she herself have been so blind that she hadn't noticed her relationship was in trouble? Even so, what Kevin did was unacceptable and forgiveness was inconceivable. Was it possible she had also been at fault? Maybe if she had spent more time with him instead of working so much, he might not have gone looking for happiness elsewhere. Then she wouldn't be lying here on the couch with this hollow aching heart and pounding head. But, if he had really loved her and wanted to stay together, he would have expressed his feelings and maybe they could've worked on their relationship.

Sadness overwhelmed her, she could envision it now; no

more "us or we," it would just be "I or me." Table for one, and she would be the third wheel when she went out with her coupled friends. Everybody would try and fix her up because they didn't want her to be alone. She didn't even want to get into blind dating; that was as appealing as pulling gum off her expensive heels and internet dating was right up there with the gum.

All Serena wanted to do was spend the day in her bed lavished in the comfort and security of its welcoming covers. Knowing she wasn't going to get that luxury now, Serena pushed the thought aside. She needed to go into the corporate office today. There would be emails and voice messages waiting for her and probably some personnel issues she needed to attend to. In addition to that, there were the usual ongoing daily responsibilities that came with running the family business. She had never imagined that someday she would be acting CEO of her dad's business, but after her dad's mini-stroke, she was awarded that title.

Serena thought back on that day for a bit, thank God her mom had been there and called 911 immediately. He made it to the hospital within minutes so the damage was minimal. He still went through months of painful therapy and his doctor ordered him to take a break from work for a year. It about killed him; he had always gone to work every day for the last twenty-five years, except for holidays, vacations and other leave time. Somebody had to run the business. Tess was extremely busy managing her own salon and wasn't really interested in the coffee business. She said she would just enjoy hers in a cup and giggled. So that left Serena to take on the responsibilities.

After one year, Serena had adapted into the position and taken on all of the responsibilities. There was a learning curve but her dad stood by her side as she walked through the transition. It was mostly her baby now; however, they still met on a monthly basis so Serena could give him an update. There were still some matters only he was qualified to handle. In fact, it was about time for them to get together. Note to self: call Dad and schedule a lunch and get the details about Books on the Corner that was supposed to belong to her now.

Serena slowly rose from the couch and after two cups of coffee, some more aspirin, a bite to eat, a shower, makeup lightly applied and hair styled, she went into her bedroom to find her days attire. The bed still looked so inviting, but instead Serena forced herself to the direction of her closet. If it was up to her, she would choose jeans, a sweatshirt, and tennis shoes. Getting dressed up today was as appealing as getting her teeth worked on. But she did have an image to uphold so that outfit was out. Instead, she picked out a red silk blouse(red to portray the sense of power she did not feel) and mated it with a black pin-striped skirt suit. She topped off the outfit with taupe nylons and her favorite four-inch Milano Blanco pumps. She adorned herself with diamond-stud earrings and her favorite gold-diamond heart necklace that Kevin had bought for her 27th birthday. It gave her comfort wearing something so pretty that was once a token of his love. A little spray of her soft musk, a touch of red lip gloss, a quick stop at the closet to get a light coat and Serena was ready to face the day. At least she looked like it on the outside but on the inside, she felt like a confused, heartbroken little girl.

She never imagined that losing someone you love could hurt so much. Suddenly the thought of going to the coast for the weekend sounded appealing to her. Maybe a long run on the beach would help her unravel her thoughts and she could come to some sense of normalcy. At this time, a picture of that was not clear to her. What was normal? She asked herself.

Serena barely caught the ten forty-five Max heading into downtown. She grabbed a seat by the window and sat prepared for the thirty-five minute commute that had become her normal daily routine. Usually, she spent the time checking her emails, going over her schedule and taking care of any tasks to pass the time of the mundane ride. But today, looking out the window, watching the rural countryside pass her by, she reflected back on the first time she had met Kevin. He came into her coffee shop one day. A new job assignment had brought him into the metro area and he was hoping to find a local coffee shop on his route to work. Serena found him quite handsome and delightfully sweet. Even though she wasn't looking for a relationship she enjoyed flirting with him. He was easy to talk to, laughed at her crazy comments and after many morning Lattés and several attempts of asking her out, Serena finally gave in. She had come to the conclusion he probably wasn't a serial killer and accepted his invitation for dinner. They went to her favorite Italian restaurant; the same one where he had proposed to her a year ago. Serena, feeling an overwhelmed sense of sadness as she took a small step back in time, laid her heavy head back against the seat and closed her tired eyes. The next thing she remembered was hearing her stop being announced.

Serena reached into her bag and discovered that she had left her walking shoes at home. Now she would have to make the four block trip in heels, her feet were definitely not going to be her friends. They were certainly going to make a point to tell her about it later that night. Getting off the train, she felt the sun on her face and thought to herself, at least the weather was beautiful, that was a plus.

Serena stood outside staring up at her office on the second floor; she needed a few moments to regroup before going in. Her dad had bought the little building over twenty-five years ago. It had been an old run-down two-story building in the heart of downtown Portland, but he had a vision. After many months of sweat and hard labor, he brought his vision to life. It still stood sturdy and proud today with its outside face, a mixture of terracotta and gray brick, and the red clay tile roof adding the finishing touch.

Serena retrieved the key from her purse and sighed before going in, she wasn't sure she was ready to face anybody or felt like answering any questions. Going through the motions, she inserted her key into the locked door. Serena, her dad and any special staff had keys, otherwise; to get access into the building, you pushed the buzzer and were escorted in. She unlocked the double glass doors and walked into the marble-lined corridor. Serena had always loved coming into the office; the inside had a charming array of architectural character. She was happy her dad had kept the unique style definition of arches and columns. A few feet in front of her an elevator took you to the second floor, or if you were feeling energetic, the spiral staircase off to the left was always an option. Sitting slightly right of the elevator was an antique hand forged Moroccan coffee pot in brass and copper, that sat atop a three-foot carved marble pedestal of black and gold. Adjacent to the elevator, on the wall were pictures proudly displaying past and present employees, special plaques and awards. She marveled at her parent's creativity, the building was like a small museum.

Serena usually took the stairs but today she opted for the elevator since her feet were already complaining. Arriving at her floor, Serena stepped out of the elevator into a small corridor onto a brushed brown carpet, surrounded by dusty cream painted walls. Directly in front of her was her dad's pride and joy; a wall containing artifacts and history of the coffee industry, there was even a picture of Mr. Coffee himself, Juan Valdez. To the right of the wall there was a glass door with the words Mike and Family Inc., etched in gold lettering.

Stepping through the door, Serena was greeted by Nina with a hot cup of coffee. She was a couple years younger and a bit shorter than Serena, took pride in her in health, and worked hard to keep her petite body fit. She was a pretty girl, her blond hair barely touched her shoulders and her long bangs she wore off to the side, played peek-a-boo with her right eye. She always came to work professionally dressed, kept the office in order and was always there for Serena.

Nina smiled and gave her friend a comforting hug. "Sorry to hear you're going through some rough times," Nina said, as she handed Serena her coffee. "I talked with Tess and she told me Kevin left you. She kept the conversation very brief and didn't go into details. We can go have a drink and talk tonight after work if you feel up to it?"

"Thank you, I'll let you know later," Serena replied, as she received a stack of messages in her other hand from Nina, and headed into her office.

Nina took a sip of her coffee, then followed Serena into her office. "Your dad called twice and wants you to call him; I told him you would be in later," she informed her.

Serena briefly scanned through the messages. "Is this all the messages?" Serena asked, glancing up at Nina.

"Yes, were you expecting more?" Nina asked.

Serena looked out the window of her two-story office and sadly remarked, "I guess it was wishful thinking on my part, even though the thought of taking him back is inconceivable, I would love to see him grovel a little bit, hmm maybe a lot."

Nina gave Serena a light pat on shoulder as she left her office. "I will be out here if you need me," Nina said.

Serena was touched by Nina's concern. Looking up she gave her friend a weak smile. "Thank you, Nina, just knowing you're here makes me feel a little better. I'll let you know about tonight," Serena promised.

3) THE UNEXPECTED ENCOUNTER

After Serena got settled into her office, she started going through her emails and voice messages. Coming across the message from her dad, reminded her, she needed to call him. That thought encouraged a little smile on her solemn face. Serena was always happy to hear his voice; she had been so terrified when he had taken ill. She felt blessed every time she had a chance to talk with him.

Serena's Dad, Mike, answered her call on the fourth ring and greeted his daughter in his usual loving voice. "Hi sweetie! I was just thinking about you. How's my girl doing?"

After a pause and a big sigh, Serena answered. "Well, you probably heard from Tess that Kevin found someone else and broke up with me. I'm still in shock and feeling a little numb; I keep reliving that morning and trying to make sense of it all," Serena admitted.

"Yes, Tess did mention something about it to me and I am so sorry to hear that," Mike said, trying to console his broken-hearted daughter. "If you ask me," he continued, "you're too good for him, and someday he will wake up and realize what he had lost. I know this is not what you wanted to hear, but Serena honey, you're strong and you'll get through this."

"Thanks Dad for the vote of confidence, you're probably right and when my heart awakens to the realization of that, things will be right with me again. Until then, it's going to be a rough road. It's not easy to throw away the three years Kevin and I spent together, and despite what happened, I can also see all the good times we had. I think that's what hurts me the most." Serena admitted to her dad, while trying to hide the storms of emotions brewing inside her. She wanted to be strong, but at the same time, Serena wished she was wrapped in his loving, caring arms, protecting her from all the hurt in the world, like he had done when she was a little girl.

"Dad," Serena continued after working to pull herself together. "Did you think we belonged together? Did you and Mom see something I didn't?"

"Serena dear," Mike said, searching for just the right words to answer his fragile daughter's question. "It's not up to me to be the judge of that. He seemed like a nice enough young man, had a decent job and from where I stood, it looked like he loved you. I accepted him because he was good to you and made you happy. I do, however, want to let you in on a little secret," Mike admitted. "According to a father, no man is ever good enough for his little girl, but your mom and I would've welcomed him into the family if you had married him."

"Now I do have to tell you, Serena," Mike continued. "I am disgusted with him and I have absolutely no respect for the man. Maybe it's a blessing it happened to you now instead of later, when you were married and had children. It's obvious he has trouble with devotion and commitment. He had better not ever show his face around here again if he knows what's best for him!"

Serena heard a hint of anger in his voice that she was not accustomed to. The last thing she wanted to do was get him upset and cause him any stress. It wouldn't be good for his present condition. She needed to reassure him that she'd be okay, then move onto a new topic. "Dad, I love you so much and thanks for listening to me. I know it's going to take some time for me to get through this. I appreciate your caring words of wisdom, but if it's okay with you, I don't want to talk about it anymore. Can we please move onto something less depressing?"

Mike submitted to his daughter's request. He could sense this was a hard thing for her to talk about. "Sure honey, what would you like to talk about?" Mike asked.

"Well... I would like to know more about the bookstore." Serena answered, glad to be talking about something else. "What can you tell me about it, and are you sure it's really mine?"

"Yes dear it is, and as far as I know, all you have to do is meet with an attorney and go over some paperwork, sign some legal documents and it's yours. It's up to you whether you want to sell it or keep it," answered Mike.

"I still can't believe it. I don't know anything about running a bookstore. Why would she choose me?" Serena asked.

"It's really no surprise, you were always Aunt Caroline's favorite, and she knew she could trust you and it would be in good hands. Running a bookstore couldn't be that much different that running a coffee shop, you're smart and have a degree in business. I know you'll figure it out. You don't have to make any decisions now; go down and check it out and think on it. As I see it, we could expand on the coffee shop inside. You were looking for new location for another shop anyway," answered Mike.

"Yes I was looking, but more in the Portland area. I even had a couple places picked out," Serena admitted. "Astoria is a little out of my range, but it so happens, dear sweet Tess talked me into driving down with her this weekend. I'm not sure I want to live down there when most of my family is here, but we'll see what happens," Serena said, pondering the thought of leaving the Rose City. "Do you know where I might get the keys?" Serena asked her Dad.

Mike was drawn to a little sadness himself when he thought of his daughter moving away. Trying to cover it with a slight cough, he answered Serena. "Yes, your Aunt gave me a set for safe keeping. Your cousin Lucy should be there during working hours and she may even have an extra set. Just to make sure you can get into the shop, stop by the house on your way and I'll give you the keys I have. Mom and I would love to see you both," answered Mike.

"Thanks, Dad, we'll probably be there around nine. However, we can't stay too long, I am hoping to make it to the coast before noon." Serena answered hoping that did not upset her Dad.

"I will let your mom know about Saturday; she isn't going to be happy about the short visit, but let me talk to her, help her see reason," Mike said.

"Thanks, you're awesome." Serena crossed her fingers in hopes that he was successful. Her mom could be pretty stubborn at times. Good luck Dad, she thought to herself with a smile. "Enough of me," Serena continued. "Let's talk about you for a while. How are you feeling?" Serena asked.

Mike answered his daughter after a slight hesitation. "According to my doctor, I'm making progress, but he still wants me to wait another year before returning to work." Mike paused, and after a heavy sigh, he continued "It just seems like it's taking so long and between you and me, sometimes I feel like I am taking two steps forward and one step back," admitted Mike. "I was hoping to be back to work by now. I'm not ready to retire yet." Mike added.

Serena felt a pang of sadness for her dad. "The doctor isn't telling you to retire, even though it does feel like it to you. It just sounds like he wants you to give it a little more time." Serena told him, hoping he could see the reason. "It's going to take time, I know it's hard to adjust when you have been used to working all your life. A year isn't too long; the doctor said you're making progress so it can only get better," Serena said, trying to sound convincing. "Maybe you can talk him into letting you work part time," commented Serena, hoping to boost her dad's spirits. "Hey, How is your boat building business going, have you made your first million yet?" Serena asked, changing the subject.

Mike laughed at his daughter's pun and commented, "It's moving along; I got another five orders yesterday. Wouldn't think they would be in such demand but there are a lot of people who like to collect them, and others who buy them as gifts. Go figure." Her dad had started building boats in a bottle and selling them on online a few months after his stroke to keep from going crazy. He was never a person that sat around, always had to be doing something. He was making a little money which he set aside for his granddaughters, and it kept him busy and out of her mom's hair. He also admitted to her that it gave him an escape from the honey-do-list. To Serena, it looked like such a tedious job and didn't know how he found any enjoyment in it. But it made him happy and that's what mattered.

The conversation between father and daughter continued flowing smoothly, business details were discussed, appointments scheduled, miscellaneous items were negotiated and they briefly touched on family matters. After the exchange of I love you, they ended the call. Serena was in better spirits and was glad she had called her dad first. Hopefully, the rest of her day would be just as rewarding.

Serena spent the next few hours answering emails, returning phone calls and joined a conference call with all the managers to discuss an upcoming book-signing tour, to be held throughout the stores. More mail was handled along with additional emails and last minute phone calls. It had been a productive day, lots accomplished and the busy work kept her from thinking about Kevin.

The more Serena pondered Nina's invite, the better it sounded. Finally conceding, she agreed to meet her after work. They ended up at a little bar and grill, not too far, just a block down from the office. Good thing too because Serena's feet would've protested a long distance hike in her heels; she still had to get home and her feet were an essential part of the task.

Serena passed on a drink, decided on water and a grilled chicken salad with a side of fruit. Nina sipped on her Margarita and munched on complimentary chips and dip while Serena filled her in on the last two days. She had just taken a drink and almost lost it when she noticed Serena shove the menu close to her face and shrieked, "Oh Shit!" With a shocking look on her face, she peeked around the side of the menu at her friend, who was now wiping up her drink from the table. "I'm sorry about that, but Kevin just sat down with a gorgeous female. Nina, promise me," Serena begged, grasping her friends arm across the table. "Please don't turn around, I'll let you know when the coast is clear." Acting as nonchalant as possible, Serena craned her neck as far as she could without falling out of her seat. She wanted to get a good look at her replacement. Softly she whispered to Nina "I wanted to see what a Ferrari looked like, and oh boy Nina, she is a top-of-the-line Luxury model; fully loaded series plus all the special features. What had he even seen in me? I am a Suburban, and an outdated one at that." Serena exclaimed.

Serena had to admit his new love was beautiful; long blond hair, petite slim figure, and dressed as if she had just stepped out of a page from a glamour magazine. Serena thought she herself, looked like a page from Home and Garden. There was absolutely no comparison.

Nina pleaded in a hushed whisper, "I want to see."

"Not yet, he might see you." Serena exclaimed.

Nina sat back in her chair and asked with one brow raised and her head slightly cocked, "Serena, are you going to hide behind that menu all night? "The waiter has walked by three times and doesn't know whether to take your order again or just leave the crazy lady alone." Nina giggled.

Peeking around the side of the menu, Serena answered her friend, "I don't want Kevin to see me. I just can't face him now," Serena admitted. "Why did he have to show up here and why is he parading her around so soon?" Serena questioned. "His presence is still permeating my house and my mind is whirling with fresh memories of us. You'd of thought there was some waiting period that needed to expire; the nerve of him." A disgusted Serena stated to no one in particular.

Serena continued watching their table until she witnessed Kevin get up and leave. She then turned her attention back to Nina. "He's gone, turn slowly around, you can't miss her."

Nina studied her for a short time and turned back to face Serena. "Maybe she's all looks and no brains. She is pretty, but with a fake undertone. Nina reached across the table and put her hand on Serena's arm, "But you Serena, are a beautiful classy lady." I am so sorry you had to witness this, you deserve so much better than that jerk," Nina said. "Would you like to take your food to go and slip out quietly?"

Serena nodded at her friend, and it was right then she realized she needed to get away. Seeing Kevin with someone else was heart wrenching, and avoiding an encounter, when they both visited the same venues, was almost impossible. Astoria was looking like a perfect escape haven.

Serena paid the check then she and Nina slipped out unnoticed. They said their goodbyes and embraced in a friendly hug. Serena vowed to meet Nina again and apologized for cutting the evening short. Her feet were under protest so she hailed a cab to the Max train to accommodate their demands. She should be home by nine and into her awaiting bed, gliding into dreamland by ten. That was, if Kevin wasn't lingering in her thoughts. Serena was so tired; she didn't want to think or do, just wanted to fall into a peaceful dreamless sleep.

Serena spent the rest of the week trying to get through each day. Work kept her busy and her mind off Kevin. The evenings were the hardest; most nights she went home, ate a light meal and surrendered to a restless sleepless night. She had finally gotten the nerve to call her wedding planner and sadly told her that her services were no longer needed, and to cancel all plans. What did make her feel a little better was that Kevin was out the deposit money. Serves him right, she said to herself. Tess checked in on her every evening. They kept their conversation short and their topics light. Wednesday they discussed their weekend plans and Tess informed Serena that Tom had an appointment that weekend, so she would be bringing Crissy and Stephanie.

Serena made herself a note to check with the Chamber of Astoria for places to take the girls. She made reservations at a quaint bed and breakfast cabin along the river and it would be awaiting their arrival Saturday afternoon.

By Friday, Serena was looking forward to the weekend. She would be on the road at eight, pick up Tess and the girls, grab the keys at her parents and then they would be coastal bound. Their senses would be infused by the refreshing coastal air by noon. She packed a light bag of clothes, some accessories and toiletries. She included both a light and a heavy coat just to be prepared, this being Oregon, you just never knew what the weather was going to do. After running through her checklist one last time, she decided to call it a day.

The next morning Serena was up early so she could allow herself a little extra time to get ready. After her morning coffee, she finished some last minute packing, threw together a few snacks for the trip, and had her Subaru loaded and ready to go. She loved driving her SUV so she opted to be chuffer. Besides, it had recently been serviced and needed to venture out of the garage. It was a safe and comfortable ride; the girls loved the TV in back and she loved the butt-warmer seats. Definitely a selling point for sure.

Fifteen minutes down the road Serena pulled into her sister's driveway located in a gated community with well-maintained lawns. Serena just loved their spacious four bedroom, two bath, ranch style home. . They had it custom built a couple years after they were married The house was surrounded and encased in a lush and beautiful landscaped yard. The grounds, both front and back, were covered in a thick blanket of rich green grass. Stepping stone paths wandered through the yard to protect its beauty. From the driveway, the view held a snake shaped brick walkway that traveled up to the porch entrance. On the right of the walkway stood a big birch that offered a bit of shade from the late day sun. From the view inside, looking out the front bay window, were Tess's prize rose bushes. In early summer, the pink, red, orange and yellow assortment insured the perfect balance of color. At the top of the five step porch, two hanging pots containing a variety of rainbow colors accented the door on each side. Walking up the steps, Serena took in the sight before her. A beveled glass door was centered between to gas sconce lanterns, when lit, casted a romantic glow on the wrap-around porch. Maybe someday she would have a house like this, Serena thought stopping at the door.

Serena rang the bell and waited. A half-dressed Tess greeted her at the door while at the same time looking over her left shoulder, telling Stephanie to find her boot. Serena scooted inside and looked around at the foyer at Tess's latest decorating updates, she was always changing something. There was a new coat rack in the corner holding an array of scarves, hats and book bags. The foyer and hallway had just been newly painted and the color complemented her dark cherry furniture perfectly. Leave it to Tess, to know exactly how to match the furniture to the colors, Serena thought. Serena followed Tess into the living room where Stephanie, who was laid back on the couch pouting and crying, didn't seem at all interested in looking for her boot. Poor Tom was patiently trying to coax his tearful daughter into a search and rescue mood. "Welcome to my everyday chaotic life, "As you can see this is somewhat mellow." Tess stated calmly. "Occasionally both girls are screaming about something and the sweet dear puppy lying at your feet," Tess motioned to Chaos, their golden retriever puppy. "He will add to the craziness by leaving a present in the hall and usually one of the girls will find it. That leads to another dramatic escapade. Thank goodness we have hardwood floors throughout the house for easy clean up. I am just grateful he is being a good puppy today, and the lost boot is the only drama we have experienced so far this morning," Tess chuckled. Give me about ten minutes. Go help yourself to some freshly brewed coffee and chill for a few," Tess motioned towards the kitchen as she disappeared down the hallway.

Serena yelled back at her sister, "Don't hurry sis; we have a little time and a cup of coffee sounds superb. I forgot to stop on my way over so I think I'll go indulge." Following the aroma, she headed for the kitchen that was located in the rear of the house. It held the normal appliances and gadgets, had more than enough cupboards done in light oak, and a speckled hand-tiled counter top completed the picture. Serena especially liked the large window that gave the room a very light and open feeling. Sitting at the dining room table drinking coffee, was always a pleasure when she'd come over.

Serena was able to grab a couple minutes of quiet time with Tom; he had somehow escaped unnoticed temporarily. She caught him up on the last day's events; it was easy to see he was angry at Kevin but he kept his frustration to a mild simmer. He and Kevin were never close friends, but they did hang out occasionally, and they would all go out for dinner or a movie once in a while. They talked about the family, hugs were in order and he went back out to look for the lost boot.

Left alone with her thoughts Serena pondered. Would this have been her life if Kevin and she had gotten married? She wondered if Kevin was father material. They had never talked of having kids but Serena had given it a thought on occasion. He had adapted well to her nieces, seemed to enjoy them when they stayed at their house for the weekend. Oh well, she thought, not her worry, it would be another woman's story to tell.

Twenty minutes later, her SUV loaded with the kids and her sister, Serena continued her adventure. She turned to her sister and teasingly said, "I obviously didn't get the clothes memo," Serena stated as she glanced at her sister and nieces. All of whom were wearing leggings, boots and long sweaters. She was dressed in comfort in her jeans, tennis shoes and an oversized sweatshirt. They looked like they were ready for a photo shoot. She felt so frumpy compared to them; it was definitely time for a change.

Tess laughed as she commented on her sister's statement. "I guess I forgot to send it to you, besides you never wear leggings, at least I have never seen you in them."

Serena thought before she answered, maybe it was time for a change. Her life was heading in a different direction, maybe her style could too. "No, I don't have any, but maybe it's time to move from suburbia and climb aboard the fashion train. Would you be willing to help me pick out some clothes and pass on some tips, sweet sister?"

Tess, excited to help Serena, answered. "Of course, I would love to. I thought you would never ask. Maybe we could stop at the outlet mall on the way back; it would be like therapy shopping. You could use it and I wouldn't mind picking up a new sweater. What do you say, is everyone up for shopping tomorrow?" Tess yelled out and the car filled with screams of excitement. "A new adventure and a transformation; this is what you need to soothe a heartache," Tess exclaimed.

"Could be," Serena apprehensively replied, wondering if she was taking on too much, too fast.

Shortly after they left Tess's, Serena heard a small voice in the back call out to her. "Aunt Sena, Mom told us that we are not supposed to talk about Kevin so we won't this whole weekend," Crissy promised. Stephanie snapped at her sister, "Cris, Mom said not to say his name. We don't want Aunt Sena to go crazy."

"Sorry Aunt Sena." Crissy apologized and through the rearview mirror Serena witness each girl make a zipper mouth and silence returned to the back seat. With her left eyebrow raised, Serena turned to her sister. Busted! "Really," she said.

Tess shrugged her shoulders and admitted, "That's not exactly how I phrased it, and I might have mentioned the word crazy in passing," Tess confessed, glancing out the window to hide the grin on her face.

4) MOVING ON

When they were a within a few miles of her parent's house, Serena made an announcement to the girls. "We are going to stop at grandma and grandpas, but only for a short visit. I am hoping to be in Astoria before noon," Serena said, glancing in the rearview mirror. "So girls, when we say it's time to go, I don't want to hear any whining about shutting off the video game. Is that understood?"

"Yes, Aunt Sena," the girls echoed.

Tess turned to her sister, "Serena dear, the girls aren't going to be the problem, you know it's going to be our dear mom. She will try and pull us into her vortex and keep us held hostage while she updates us with everyone's lives, even the additional nine lives from the cat down the street." Tess laughed.

Serena knew Tess was right. She loved her parents dearly but when it came time to say goodbye and get out the door, it could be a challenge. Her mom never used to be much of a gossiper, usually she would keep family drama and private matters to herself. But that all changed when her dad had his stroke. She found comfort in her social groups and making new friends. It helped to endure her lonely nights at home while her husband was at the rehabilitation facility. The problem was, now she thought everyone should be informed of her latest findings. At times Serena sat starry-eyed, nodding her head while her mom talked at the speed of sound about all these people Serena didn't know. She was pretty sure her mom didn't know all of them either. She definitely had contact with way too many people. "Maybe I shouldn't have introduced Mom to social media. It was probably a big mistake." Serena admitted.

"You think?" Tess remarked.

"Well it wasn't my fault entirely," stated Serena. "If memory serves, we both agreed that getting Mom connected to a social media group would be a smart idea. It was supposed to be used to keep the family and their friends informed on Dad's progress during recovery. I guess neither of us imagined she'd get so attached and make so many friends. I can't believe she has close to two hundred now," Serena stated, shaking her head. "Maybe when the newness wears off she will find something else to occupy her spare time."

"Hopefully sooner than later," Tess stressed. "I have a hard time deciding on what to share with Mom because she gets post happy and there are some things I'd like to keep private."

"Hey Mom," Stephanie called from the backseat. "What is a vortex and why is grandma going to pull you and Aunt Sena into it?"

Serena turned to her sister with a smile and quietly spoke.

"Out of the mouths of the babes, it's all yours sis."

Tess gave her sister a fake smile and turned her attention to her daughter, "Stephanie honey, it's kind of like a dryer. You know how you put clothes in it and it goes around and around until it stops. Well, that's like a vortex and I was just being funny so let's just keep this our little secret, okay?" Tess said in an attempt to answer her daughter, praying they wouldn't say anything to her mom, and crossing her fingers for extra luck.

Stephanie gave her mom an okay and went back to reading her book she had brought with her.

"Really Tess," Serena giggled. "A dryer, is that the best you could do?"

The look Tess gave Serena would probably have been followed by the finger if the girls hadn't been in the car. So Serena decided she should zip her own mouth shut and drive.

Serena turned into her parents driveway lined in gravel, and on each side, rows of fir trees guided you to their home hidden by more trees. They lived in a two-story house designed in country flair. Besides the trees, varieties of plants, shrubbery and flowers gave welcome to the big front yard. On the porch sat a wicker sofa and chair accompanied by lavish pillows with heavy color and pattern, and joining them two potted ferns that overflowed in their large ornate vases. In her younger years, Serena sat up there many nights, lost in thought while enjoying a warm summer breeze.

The inside invited you in with a decorative style that was casual but tasteful. The furniture gave warmth to the surroundings and had been selected from local antique dealers. Most finds had been refurbished and needed little work; others her father had taken much pleasure in restoring. Family pictures of past and present, gave life to the walls around them. Serena found her dad sitting in his favorite wooden Windsor rocking chair, enjoying his morning coffee and catching up on the news. Her mom, Alice, was perched at the desk with the mouse attached to her hand, deeply engrossed in a story on the computer.

The girls, after a visit to the bathroom, ventured into the living room and planted themselves on the camel back sofa, centered on a braided area rug. They were hoping to con grandpa into setting up the video system for them. The score was girls; 2; grandpa 0.

With the greetings out of the way, the adults headed towards the kitchen. Before they were out of the living room, Tess heard Stephanie call out, "Grandma, are you taking Mom and Aunt Sena to the vortex?"

Before Alice could turn to go back into the living room to answer her granddaughter's strange question, Tess grabbed her arm and directed her to the kitchen and laughed. "Mom, that is a word on her spelling list, she was trying it out. You know those girls, always being funny, so how about some of that coffee..." Tess said, while leading her towards the kitchen, hoping to distract her. In the future she was going to have to be more aware of what she said around those girls.

They entered the kitchen through an arched doorway into a very spacious open room. It had just been updated with all the latest stainless steel appliances and tiled flooring. Oak cupboards framed the area, and light brown marble gave life to the counters. Below the kitchen window was a stainless steel double sink and in the center of the room, Serena's favorite part of the kitchen, sat a large built-in island below her mom's sterling silver hanging pots and pans. Her parents took pride in their home and every room added something to it. The kitchen, however, was her mom's favorite room. She loved to cook and bake so her dad had designed her mom the dream kitchen she'd always wanted. Serena could smell the freshly baked cherry and apple pies fresh out of the oven. She could almost taste the lingering sweetness of the frosting drizzled cinnamon rolls, sitting on the counter.

A beautiful rectangular antique oak kitchen table with hand carved legs and matching chairs invited you over to enjoy a family meal, or to just sit and chat. It was adorned with a lace table cloth and a nice bouquet that pulled attention to it. Serena set the table while her mom and Tess prepared the coffee and set out the cinnamon rolls. They then sat down and each took part in sharing the latest happening in their everyday life. Alice, of course, talked about her friends; Mike about how his boat business was going and some politics. Tess shared a bit about Tom and the girls and Serena spoke very little about Kevin and what happened between them. They were all in agreement when she wanted to change the subject. Serena happened to glance up at the rooster clock on the wall and noticed it was almost nine-thirty. At that, she announced they needed to get going to beat the traffic.

"Do you have to leave now?" Alice asked with a whine. "Surely you can stay a little longer, I can make you a real breakfast, you haven't heard all the latest news and I want to spend time with my grandbabies," she pleaded.

Serena gave Tess a distressed look; she didn't want to hurt her mom's feelings but they had plans and she was anxious to get on the road. Sweet Tess came to the rescue. "As much as we would like to stay, we just can't. We have reservations and promised the girls we would take them sightseeing. We will have to take a rain check," Tess exclaimed.

Good for you Tess, Serena thought. Nice touch mentioning the girls. Tess knew how much her mom cherished those babies and she wouldn't want them to be disappointed.

Part of Serena felt bad and maybe a little guilty because she wasn't staying a little longer. It had been awhile since she had been out to her childhood home, and she couldn't deny that fact that her parents were getting older. Where had the time gone? She thought to herself. They were both in their late fifties, although they didn't look like it. For the last few years her mom had started cooking healthier meals and encouraged her dad to take daily walks with her. Serena could see the reflection of Tess in her mom, just an older version, showing a few wrinkles around the face and a little gray, which she kept hidden by her six-week visit to the beauty shop. Her dad standing at 6'1" was still quite handsome. Serena noticed, however, his soft brown hair was getting a little thin on top and a hint of gray was peeking through it. She could see a glimpse of the after effects of the stroke, which seemed to still haunt her.

"I'll try and come by next Saturday for dinner." Serena said, nudging her sister.

Tess gave her a discrete disgusted look and solemnly added apprehensively. "We probably can make it too." They all agreed on four o'clock which seemed to satisfy her parents. They engaged in a few more minutes of small talk, and then her parents spent a little time trying to talk to the girls, which wasn't easy competing with the video game. Mike gave Serena the keys, and Alice handed her a container filled with baked goods, and they were out the door in record time after hugs and loves.

"Did you have to include me in your dinner plans?" Tess asked none too happy. "Tom is okay with special occasions and holidays, but Mom and Dad tend to overwhelm him sometimes. He isn't going to like it and he is going to make it a point to tell me," Tess complained.

"Tess I needed more strength. I wasn't enough," Serena stated, pleading her defense. "I figured it would make her happy if we both came to dinner. You do have to admit, it did work," Serena commented, as she looked at her sister with puppy eyes.

"Well, you owe me one sister. It might be just me and the girls unless I can bribe Tom into coming." Tess submitted.

"Point taken. I am sorry for pulling you in. It really wasn't fair but I was running out of options. Serena apologized.

"I'll make it up to you tomorrow at the mall, will that help?"

"Well, it's a start." Tess said with a pouty voice.

Serena celebrated to herself, all right, point back.

After leaving her parents' house, they were finally on their way and by the time they merged onto Highway Twenty Six heading west, the girls had fallen asleep which gave Tess and Serena some quality time to talk. The girls, when they weren't sleeping, spent time reading or watching a movie on the little TV. Once in a while they would engage in the conversation and talk about their friends and school. They even managed to talk their mom and aunt into playing the license plate game. All in all it was a fun trip, and even with the two rest stops they arrived in Astoria close to twelve thirty. Serena was hoping she could check into their cabins before four o'clock.

As luck would have it, they were able to check in early. It was picture perfect overlooking the water, and since it was rented sight unseen, it was a relief to see the beauty of the cabin and surroundings had matched the picture she had seen on the net. After checking in and unpacking, they dined on fresh seafood in a restaurant down by the dock, took the girls to see a couple of favorite children's attractions in town, then headed over to the bookstore.

Before going in, Serena stood outside looking up at the vertical sign that gave notice to the quaint little store on the corner. The letter K was burned out so the sign read "Boo s on the Corner." Note to self: have that fixed first thing, before inebriated tourists think it was a place to purchase alcohol. That was if she took over ownership. They arrived before it closed so Serena didn't need the keys; they would however, come in handy if she wanted to check it out on her own during non-working hours.

Lucy, her cousin, was helping a customer when they walked in. She looked up and greeted them with a loving smile. "Well, look at what the cat dragged in," Lucy said teasingly. "Your dad said I would be seeing you, I was hoping you would make it here before closing. Give me a minute to finish with this customer and I'll be right with you. Tess, you can let the girls play in the children's area. It's just to the right of the Fiction section, there are some puzzles, toys and lots of books to keep them occupied," Lucy stated, pointing in that direction.

While waiting for her cousin, Serena took in her surroundings; she had to admit it was a cute little shop. Lots of crowded shelves packed with books made walkways throughout the store, every section was clearly labeled. Comfy chairs sat by a large stained glass window. A perfect hideaway for customers to sit and indulge in a latté while temporarily escaping into their favorite read. A display case filled with gifts, mermaid sculptures, and pewter whales were waiting for a collector to claim their treasures. And jewelry made by the local artists sparkled in a showcase on the counter. There was even a chair and sofa in the children's corner surrounded by pillows; where Serena imagined a storyteller sitting and sharing a favorite fantasy-filled story, while a young starry-eyed audience sat clinging to every word.

The question though, could she see herself here? Was this the place for her? Lucy, who was eight years older than Serena, was born and raised in Astoria. Her dad died when she was quite young from a boating accident while fishing. So, for many years, it was just Lucy and Caroline. Lucy would help out in the shop on occasion; when she had a break from college and holidays. While attending college she met Brad; the man of her dreams. He proposed to her a week after she graduated. He was able to get a decent job in Astoria which pleased them both. They agreed it would be a perfect place to start a family and it would be close to her mom. Lucy had been successfully managing the shop on her own ever since her mom lost her two-year battle with cancer. Serena wondered if she could make the shop her own and fill the shoes of such two amazing ladies. It wasn't going to be easy.

It had been awhile since Serena had seen Lucy; she had cut her long hair, and the short bob hairstyle suited her and accented her beautiful face. She had lost most of the weight she had gained with the birth of her twin boys, and was looking good in her comfortable 'I love Astoria' sweatshirt, leggings, and boots. Serena thought to herself, what's up with leggings and boots? Was she the only one that didn't get the memo?

Finished with her customer, Lucy walked over to Tess and Serena. "Welcome to Books on the Corner ladies! Come here and let me look at the two of you," Lucy said, opening her arms wide, inviting them in for a hug. "It's so good to see you both, and Tess your girls are so adorable. The spitting image of their beautiful mother," complimented

Lucy.

"Thank you; they are a handful at times but they're pretty good girls most of the time. It's good to see you too Lucy; you're looking beautiful as ever," Tess said, returning the compliment. "You certainly don't look like you just had twins, and I bet those boys are growing like weeds. What are they now, about four?" Tess asked.

Lucy gave a loving smiled, then answered. "Working here keeps me on my feet and that has helped me shed some of those unwanted pounds, and chasing the boys helps me keep it off," She laughed. "Jason and Justin are four and a half to be exact. I would love for you to see them while you are here, that is, if you have time."

"Probably can't make that happen this trip but let's agree to get together next time we're in town," Tess said, looking forward to seeing her boys

"How about you Serena, how are you holding up? Lucy asked. "Sorry to hear about you and Kevin, I always thought you two would marry and raise a family. He is totally a fool for leaving you. You know I'm just a phone call away if you need someone to talk to."

"Thanks, Lucy, I have your number and I might take you up on that," Serena replied, then added, "To answer your question, I also thought he was my forever man, but it turned out I wasn't his forever girl. Thank goodness for Tess. She has been my saving grace and sounding board. To get through the pain I try to take it one day at a time, some days are harder than others. I've found that staying busy helps keep my mind from wandering."

Lucy gave Serena a comforting hug and changed the subject. "Well, I guess I probably should give you a tour before it gets too late. You've seen most of the ground floor, except for the coffee shop in the back and the two bedroom apartment upstairs, which is currently used for storage. Let me first lockup; it's just about time and besides I would feel better with the girls here. They can continue playing while we look around. We have never had any problem, 'but better safe than sorry' I always say," commented Lucy. "I'll show you the upstairs first," Lucy said, motioning Serena and Tess to the staircase at the end of the hall.

"I was unaware of this apartment," Serena stated as they entered the small quarters. Thinking to herself, this could be her solution to finding a place to stay; that was, if she took over ownership and the quarters were livable.

"Yes, it's quite cute," stated Lucy, as she searched for the main light switch. "As you can see, it does need a little tender care and all the boxes need to be put in the basement. It has one bath complete with shower and tub directly off the main bedroom, fully plumbed and a gas furnace. Besides the main bedroom, there is another small room that can be used as a bedroom or office. Of course, no home is complete without the kitchen-dining-room combo and a cozy living room. I think it's only about nine hundred square feet. Mom would rent it out to college students on occasion," Lucy added.

The apartment was small, but Serena could see a lot of

potential there. A deep cleaning and a little paint would surely freshen up the little place. She really didn't need much room, and her furniture would look perfect here. Serena realized that she was leaning towards the possibility of moving here and taking over the shop. Tess was right; it could be just what she needed for a brand new start. "New starts are always good," came an unfamiliar voice. "What was that?" Serena asked. With a shrug of their shoulders neither Tess nor Lucy admitted to saying a word. It must have been somebody on the street below, Serena thought, only a quick glance out the window proved that there didn't seem to be a soul in sight. Maybe I imagined it, Serena thought.

"Oh Serena, this would be just perfect for you. I could help you fix it up and I know Tom would help you move. What do you think, Sis?" Tess asked after surveying the apartment.

Serena had to admit that the shop was slowly growing on her and a change would do her good. "I'd like to see the coffee shop before I make a final decision," stated Serena. "I'll meet you both there. I'm going out to the car to get my journal to write down all these ideas I have reeling in my head. See you in a quick sec," Serena promised.

The cold brisk air had hit Serena unexpectedly and of course, she had forgotten to grab her jacket. So in the urgency of wanting to escape from the cold as quickly as possible, she hurried to the car. However, she didn't notice the dip in the sidewalk but her foot happened to find it for her. This sent her off balance, and thinking to herself as she was falling, this wasn't going to be pretty. The next thing she remembered was being engulfed in strong arms, wrapped tightly around her from behind. It must have been worse than expected. She must have died and gone to heaven because as she looked up, she saw this handsome angel smiling down upon her. He had the most beautiful baby blue eyes she had ever seen.

Serena didn't know how long she stayed frozen in that state, it seemed like forever. It was a pleasant place with a spectacular view, so there were no complaints on her part. "Hello," said the angel, "are you okay?"

"Uh-huh," was all Serena could say.

"That would have been a nasty fall. Lucky for you I was walking by. The city really should fix the sidewalk. It's tripped me up a time or two, but luckily I haven't fallen." "Here, let me help you up," the angel offered.

Serena, coming to the conclusion she wasn't dead and it wasn't an angel holding her, relaxed. She let the man attempt to help her stand upright, which was fine with her, considering she was having a hard time balancing on her own. Her legs felt like Jell-O and butterflies were doing acrobatic stunts in her stomach. She was still a little disoriented and realized that this handsome man had saved her from hitting the ground. Although Serena could think of many reasons why she should step away from the stranger, she was content staying in his arms. Even though it was freezing outside, Serena no longer felt the cold. The tingling in her belly was making her feel warm and fuzzy.

Finally, after she found her senses, Serena parted from the stranger and turned to face him. "I owe you a thank you. Do you always rescue damsels in distress?"

"Only the pretty ones," the man answered.

For some reason, the comment made Serena blush and she shied away from the man. "I would invite you in for a coffee, but the shop is closed, maybe another time," Serena said. "I need to get back inside. My cousin and sister are waiting for me and probably wondered what's taking me so long."

The man held out his hand and said, "I'm Cliff and what might be the damsels' name."

With a smile on her face, Serena accepted his hand and told him her name. This man was handsome and also had a sense of humor. "I really need to go, maybe I'll see you around," Serena commented, as she turned to go inside.

"Oh I'm sure of it," Cliff stated, watching her disappear inside the store.

Cliff turned to walk away and in his mind relived the past few minutes. He was just finishing up giving a bid on remodeling the jewelry store up the block, and as he was heading to his truck, he witnessed a cute little redhead trip and he could see she was headed for a terrible fall.. Luckily he was just a few feet from her, and thanks to his high jump experience in school, and his everyday runs on the beach, he was able to reach her before she fell to the ground. What surprised him though, he didn't expect that he would find himself with his arms wrapped around a soft warm body, and staring into the eyes of the most beautiful girl he had ever laid eyes on. Smiling, Cliff thought to himself, this had turned out to be a good day. He got the contract and met Serena; things were looking up for him. What was he thinking; he had just ended a relationship with his ex, Tandy, who in his book, was a little on the crazy side. So what was he doing thinking of getting involved already? Maybe he wouldn't be seeing her around, it was best that he kept his distance. He didn't even know if she was available.

When Serena stepped into the store she found Tess and Lucy putting on their coat, Serena figured they were going out to look for her. "What happened to you? You were only parked out front and we got worried. You've been gone for over twenty minutes," a distressed Tess commented.

"Sorry, in my haste to get to the car, I tripped on a dip in the sidewalk and the most gorgeous man I have ever seen, helped me up. We talked for a bit and he made sure I was safe and sound, that's about it. Sorry, I took so long," Serena apologized. She didn't want to go into detail of what had happened yet. It was best to keep it to herself for now, at least until she processed through her own feelings and emotions over the encounter. A new relationship is the last thing Serena needed or wanted.

Tess suspiciously looked at her sister with a raised eyebrow and asked. "Gorgeous man?"

"Not important," Serena answered not wanting to discuss

it. She quickly looked away from her sister and changed the subject.

"Lucy," Serena stated. "It's getting late; we should have a quick look at the coffee shop and head out. It's close to dinner time and I imagine the girls and Tess are getting hungry and I could use a bite myself.'" Hearing the word dinner, the girls both ran over to the adults and stated their requests. "I want a hamburger," Stephanie pleaded. "I want pizza," added Crissy." Then the battle began. Tess broke in and said, "you'll both get peanut butter and jelly sandwiches if you don't stop this fighting. Now go back and play for a few more minutes and then we'll all discuss this." The girls, not too happy with their mothers scolding, said okay with pouty faces, and went back to play.

"Well handled Tess," Lucy stated. "I wish that worked on the twins. They just keep at it until they are sent to time out."

"It was just luck tonight. It is not always this easy, believe me." Tess replied.

Lucy led them through an arched doorway into the coffee shop. Serena was in awe of the sweet aroma of fresh roasted beans permeating the air. Her taste buds were begging for the burst of flavor.

The coffee shop was a warm and welcoming place. She could picture, on an average day, the barista behind the bar with a pleasant smile, frothing milk and pulling shots, preparing the specialty drinks for the regulars. Friends sitting around the small tables enjoying a latté while catching up on the latest gossip. A young couple would be cuddled in the corner table oblivious to their surroundings, and who could forget the businessman, on his cell closing a deal or borrowing the Wi-Fi and viewing reports on his laptop.

Serena took copious notes. Her mind working faster than her pen could write. The thoughts flowing one after another made it hard to keep up with Lucy's conversation as she showed them around the shop and pointed out important details. She could see the possibilities. It didn't need much, maybe updated equipment and a little remodeling, but for the most part, it would do.

"I love it!" Serena exclaimed while throwing her arms up wide and spinning in a circle. "Books, coffee and a home all under the same roof, also a glorious view of the river from the living room window. What more could anyone want." Serena exhaled loudly, squared her shoulders and turning to face her sister she asked, "What do you think Tess?"

With a smile at her sister's obvious enthusiasm of her new quest, Tess replied thoughtfully, "I think you should go for it. I am going to miss having you close, but I think it's a great opportunity for you." .

"There is a spare bedroom; you can all visit anytime and it would be perfect for a girl's night away," Serena added.

5) NEW BEGINNINGS

Serena, Tess, and the girls said their goodbyes to Lucy and waved ecstatically as she drove off in her Honda Pilot. The girls, who had been fairly patient up until this point, decided it was time to discuss dinner plans again, both still wanting something different. Finally in agreement, they found themselves at a little pizza parlor that also served hamburgers which made everybody happy.

By eight that evening, they were back at the cabin. Serena treated herself to a glass of white wine and stepped out onto the balcony to take in the breathtaking view, while Tess put the girls down for bed. As she gazed out into the river, Serena thought if someone had told her two weeks ago she would be moving and about to become the owner of a bookstore/coffee shop combo, she would have told them they were crazy. Her life had certainly done a one-eighty since last month. It was now up to Mr. Fate and Miss Destiny to carry her through her new phase of life. The chill of the cold caused her to move inside, where she made herself comfortable on the little sofa, pondering over the events of the day.

Tess poured herself a glass of wine, joined Serena on the sofa and said after a sigh, "whew, those girls were so exhausted they were out in minutes." "Here!" Tess said, opening her hand and placing it in Serena's. "They wanted me to give you their good night kisses."

Serena smiled as she took the pretend kisses in her hand and placed them on her cheek.

"I also called Tom," Tess said as she sipped her wine. "He said he would help you move, which should take one more thing off of your list. He has a friend down here – Griff or Biff or something like that," she stated waving her hand dismissively, "that may be willing to lend a hand. He's going to call him and see if he is available. He had been meaning to get together with him for awhile, so it would be a good opportunity for them to reconnect."

Serena peered up at her sister with a distant look in her eyes. "Thank you, Tess, and please tell Tom I am grateful for this offer."

"Is everything okay? Tess asked. "You should be happy and celebrating."

"I'm really trying," Serena said with a sigh. "It just seems so surreal, first the breakup and now this new adventure my life is taking. It seems to be happening so fast and I'm a little scared at the thought of moving so far away from my family and friends." Serena admitted, clutching her wine glass to her chest.

Tess patted her sister's leg. "Yes, I could see how it could be very overwhelming, but as soon as you get moved and settled into your new place, your life won't seem so chaotic.

You have Lucy and her family here and your good friend Rosie who lives in Seaside, which is only a few miles down the coast," Tess said, pointing in that direction, hoping to brighten her sister's outlook.

"You're right, it will be nice to spend time with Lucy and I do need to connect with Rosie. It's been awhile since we had a chance to catch up. I deserve a little girl time!" Serena admitted with a little lift in her voice. "For a while I'll be making weekly trips to the corporate office in Portland until I can find someone to manage that area, so we can arrange to meet for lunch. Speaking of which, I have been giving considerable thought to promoting Nina. She's been with the company for over ten years and it's about time to move her up the ladder. I could train her and then she can handle the responsibilities in Portland while I'm trying to adjust here. I just have to get Dad to agree to the idea." "Thanks Tess for your insight, I do feel a bit better. I am going to miss you, though."

"You'll do just fine. I am not that far away, we have a phone, text, and email, and I've always wanted to do Facetime. Also, you can stay with us when you're in town, I won't take no for an answer." At that being said, Tess raised her glass in the air and added. "Let's make a toast, to new beginnings!" "To new beginnings!" Serena echoed. The clinking sound of the glasses consummated the toast. "I also agree that Nina is perfect for the job and I don't think you'll have a problem convincing Dad of that." Tess added.

The next day Serena got up early due to a bizarre dream

that had awakened her out of a restful sleep. Cliff had found his way into her dreams, which was a little unnerving for Serena. A brief encounter from the day before certainly didn't warrant his presence in her bed at night. The problem was, her dream-self welcomed him with open arms. She would definitely need to inform her that no men visitors were allowed to invade her sleep. She was taking a break from men and relationships until she could put her life back together. The way things looked, it was going to take quite some time before that happened.

Serena decided a long run on the beach would help to clear her head. She threw on her running gear, grabbed a bottle of water, quietly slipped out and jumped into her SUV. The city was quiet, waiting it's awakening of a new day. She passed drive-thru coffee houses lined with cars as people waited for their cup-of-wake-up, and cafés and restaurants prepared for the early morning rush from tourists wanting to get an early start. Two runners gave her a friendly wave as she sat waiting for a stop light to change. So far Serena was impressed with the little city, and was looking forward to exploring her new surroundings when she got settled. The beach itself was beautiful, inviting early morning runners to bask it its glory. Serena was in her element now, running was her passion. It gave her permission to step out of reality and let her mind slip into a serene peaceful state, allowing her to put things into perspective.

Clicking her iPod to a running playlist of her favorite tunes, Serena allowed herself to get lost deep in her thoughts as her feet carried her along the sand. She was so tuned into her music and keeping up her pace that she didn't hear the man behind her calling his dog and trying to get her attention. The dog was enjoying his daily exercise and was on a dead run heading straight for her. Serena was surprised when she felt this tremendous force hit her from behind. It knocked the wind out of her and sent her sprawling to the ground.

Shaking her head Serena gently lifted herself into a sitting position to assess the damage. As she was trying to pull herself up and get her bearings, familiar strong arms wrapped around her. To make matters worse, a large golden lab was adding wet slobbery kisses to an already disgustingly gritty face. Luckily her sunglasses, no longer on her face, had kept most of the sand away from her eyes. Serena was trying to get the sand out of her mouth while attempting to push the dog away from her.

"PLEASE get this dog off me!" Serena demanded, none too happy about the fall. The dog moved away under the command of his master.

"I'm sorry about that, Brody was making sure you were okay and it's his way of apologizing," Cliff said as he helped an unhappy Serena up off the ground.

Back on her feet again, Serena pulled herself out of his arms and made an attempt to brush off the sand. "Isn't there a leash law on this beach?" Serena asked, glaring at Cliff.

Cliff trying not to stare at the disheveled sexy mess, answered Serena. "I am really sorry, Brody gets excited when I give him free rein. Normally we're the only ones out here this time of morning. I tried calling him and I called out your name but both of you just kept on running. You must not have heard me. Are you okay?" He asked, but noticing her slightly irritated mood and the shape she was in, Cliff figured that was probably a loaded question, so he prepared himself for the worst.

If looks could kill, Cliff would have been flat on the ground as Serena glared mercilessly at him. She wasn't sure if he was the last straw, or if all the pent-up hurt and anger were letting loose, but with her arms going frantically up and down and her feet pacing in front of him , Serena spewed out everything in his direction.

 "Do I look like I am? Haven't you noticed I am covered in sand, it's even in places sand should never be allowed to go. My face feels gross from your dog's slobber and the sand mixed together. I have gritty teeth and I don't even want to think about how I am going to get it out of my hair," Serena said, putting her hand on her head giving notice to the matted mess. Uncontrollable tears let loose as she continued. "To top it off; my fiancé left me, I am contemplating moving away from my family and friends and taking over a new business. So the answer to your question," Serena cried as she forcefully grabbed the towel Cliff was handing to her, "I AM NOT OKAY!" She screamed while her feet repeatedly took turns stamping in the sand.

Cliff watched Serena as she was having the little meltdown, and under the circumstances could understand her frustration and anger. The fall didn't help, but it gave her the key to open the door and let her emotions flood. He wanted to take her in his arms and make everything right, but by the looks of her current disarray, now wouldn't be a good time. He wasn't even sure he wanted to give Serena her broken sunglasses and tangled up iPod covered in sand. At the moment, he was at a loss for words, so he stood silently staring at the redheaded mess.

Serena attempted to wipe off her face, which now had tear streaks added to already icky recipe of gunk. She wasn't sure what just happened, it wasn't like her to share so much of herself to a near stranger. He probably thought she was a whack job. Serena searched for the words to describe her ludicrous out lash.

"I am terribly sorry," Serena stated. "I should never have blown up like that. It's just that my life is pulling me in so many different directions and I'm not sure which way to go." Serena took a deep breath and continued. "I've made so many changes in such a short time. I thought I had a handle on it but it's affected me worse than I thought. Please excuse my terrible outburst. Not to say that I am not still a little pissed at getting knocked down, but the rest is not your fault."

Cliff put his arm around Serena. "You don't have any reason to apologize, we all tend to take on too much too fast and overload our circuits. "Hey." Cliff said as he turned to Serena and put his hand under her chin, and guided it to face him, "Sometimes you just have to let it all go."

Mr. Fate and Miss Destiny had a bad sense of humor. This was not the direction Serena wanted to go with her life. She did not want to like Cliff. She especially didn't want to be looking into his eyes and wanting him to kiss her. She didn't want to notice he had a soft but rugged face with a tight shaved beard, just begging to be touched. He also had a small scar above his right eye and his short, wavy, chocolate brown hair, which was in a tousled mess was as sexy as hell. She needed to get away from him, so for a start, Serena stepped back to put a little distance between them.

"I really should be going," Serena announced. She had spent more time there than she had wanted, and still had one more stop to make before going back to the cabin. Cliff and Brody escorted Serena to the car, "Here, I almost forgot," Cliff said, handing her the glasses and iPod.

"Thanks," Serena said, looking at the mess placed in her hands, which contained broken Oakley's that her sister had given to her on her last birthday, and her iPod which was full of sand. Serena loved those glasses but they could be replaced; she only hoped she could get her music off of the iPod.

Cliff reached into his pocket and pulled out a business card. "Here's my card with my number in case you need to reach me. The least I can do is replace those items."

Serena took his card and without looking, set it in the seat next to her broken possessions. "Thanks, I may take you up on that," Serena said as she settled into her car. She was in a hurry to get away from this man who made her feel so vulnerable; driving past him she smiled and returned his wave.

Cliff watched Serena's taillights fade away as she headed down the road. He looked down at Brody, his three-year-old, hundred-pound yellow lab canine companion. He had rescued him when he was only a year old and they had been best buds ever since. "Why did you have to run into her, of all people?" Brody, with the saddest puppy eyes, looked up at his loyal master and friend. "Don't you give me that sad eye look; yes, I agree she is pretty and seems nice, but women are trouble. Let me refresh your memory, we just went that route and it didn't turn out good for either of us. We're doing just fine and we don't need anyone complicating our lives." Brody stood at attention tilting his head from side to side, as though he was making sense of what his master was saying. "And you traitor, I saw you covering her face with kisses." For a quick second, Cliff wondered what it would be like to hold her and kiss those irresistible lips. He immediately shook off the thought and called to Brody. "Come on boy, let's go; we got work to do and I think there is a bone in the truck with your name on it. She's trouble, so it's best if we forget all about her." He climbed up into his pickup and wondered if he was trying to convince his dog or himself. If only it was that easy, he thought.

Serena wanted to stop at the bookstore and give the apartment one last look before they had to leave. She gave Tess a quick call to inform her of her plans. She and the girls were having breakfast and then going to watch the sea lions on the docks. Serena promised to be quick. They still had to get their "shopping on" and she wanted to take the girls to the Cheese Factory on their way home.

Once inside her little apartment, Serena went directly to the bathroom and made an attempt to half way clean herself up. She still had sand particles lingering on her face and it was going to take a lot of scrubbing to get all the sand out of her hair. That would have to wait until she could take a shower at the cabin.

Standing in the living room of her soon to be new home, Serena wondered if she had made the right decision. Hadn't she read somewhere that you were supposed to wait a year or so before making any drastic changes or important decisions after a traumatic experience?

"That's just an old wives tale." An unfamiliar voice blurted out, Serena looked out the window, but just like yesterday, the corner was empty and there wasn't anybody in the shop. "Lady, come over here." The voice demanded. Great! Serena thought to herself, the voice was talking to her and reading her mind. It could only mean one thing; she was developing an alter ego, probably due to the amount of stress she had been under. Oh my goodness! What if this was the first of many voices to be living in her head. Serena sat down on the sofa. Placing her face in her hands she thought about her predicament. This was all Kevin's fault.

Before the breakup, she had been living a normal sane life and now she was sitting in a strange room, in unfamiliar surroundings, wondering if she was going crazy because she was hearing a voice, a voice with no human form connected to it. "Lady, you are not going crazy." The voice said. That's it, she was going to make an appointment to have her head examined when she returned home. But for now, she had to pull herself together or she was going to go stark raving mad and at this point that wasn't far to go. Serena found her music app on her cell phone and turned the volume up. She was hoping to drown out the voice while she went room to room measuring and making note of what needed to be done before she could move in. Satisfied with her accomplished tasks, Serena left the apartment, unaware that the voice had spoken to her one last time as she closed the door. "Please, lady, help me!"

Luckily when Serena arrived back at the cabin, Tess and the girls were still gone. She didn't want her sister to see her in this condition, she'd want an explanation and Serena didn't want to deal with that now. Tess and the girls made it back to the cabin shortly after Serena was dressed and packed. Minutes later they had the SUV loaded and were on their way home. She was sorry to be leaving the little city but would be happy to get back and start moving her life in its new direction.

The rest of the trip was dedicated to having fun. They stopped at the outlet mall where Tess helped Serena find a pair of leggings and some classy low heeled boots. She also talked Serena into buying two new shirts, a semi-tight knit sweater and pair of straight legged blue jeans. Serena kept her promise and bought Tess a new sweater and also treated her nieces to new outfits. She liked to spoil them whenever she got the chance. They ate at the Cheese Factory after taking a quick tour, and before leaving, treated themselves to an ice cream cone.

The ride back to Portland was considerably quiet. The girls

had fallen asleep a few miles out of town and even Tess was resting her eyes. Serena wondered if she would run into Cliff again. He had given her his card with his number but calling him wasn't an option. She needed to put him out of her mind. Totally not happening, not going there and definitely not interested. So why did she get excited thinking about how she felt in his strong arms and desiring more. She needed to get control of her emotions because it was obvious her body wasn't responding to her demands. Serena also realized the voice hadn't talked to her since leaving the apartment. In fact, that's the only place she had heard it. Great, she thought. Was it possible her new home was haunted? That was ridiculous, there had to be a logical explanation, only at this time she was too exhausted to think of one. She turned on the radio to soft rock and kept her mind focused on the drive home.

Early the next day, Serena was pulled from her restful sleep from a loud sound, coming from the neighbors in the apartment above her. Instead of trying to fight the noise and go back to sleep, she decided to get up and prepare for her day. After following her morning routine, Serena made herself a coffee, sat down at her kitchen table and reviewed her written task list. After weighing the urgency of each task, she put them in order of priority. Looking down at her updated list, Serena realized there was a lot that to get done in the next two weeks. If only she had a wife or better yet a clone. One of her could stay and handle matters here, and the other could start on the apartment in Astoria. Since that wasn't going to happen she went to plan B, buckled up and get it done.

At the end of the first week, Serena had managed to get most of her apartment packed. The only things left were few needed essentials. Totally exhausted from all the work, Serena sat down in her chair with a glass a wine and stared at her nearly empty apartment. Raising her glass in the air she toasted herself and celebrated her accomplishments. She had met with the attorney and was now holding the deed to The Books on the Corner. She still couldn't believe she was doing this. Her life, at this time, was contained in the boxes, stacked and categorized in three rows in her living room. One row held all her belongings that were going with her, another was going to the trash and the last held all her possessions going to Goodwill, that without Tess's help would have been in the first row. She would say, "Do you really need this?" Then Serena would reply, "Oh I can't get rid of that," then Tess would give Serena a stern look and would assertively say, "Yes, you can. What do you need it for?" If Serena didn't have a quick comeback and a valid reason, the article ended in the Goodwill pile. Serena was able to win on occasion and rescue an item that she swore had memorable value; otherwise she was forced to part with it.

Tess was right on most counts. Serena did need to de-clutter her apartment as well as her life and start out fresh. Like the cliché; out with the old and in with the new. Serena just had to keep reassuring herself of that. It did give her added satisfaction to add a box of Kevin's belongings to the Goodwill pile. It was things he had left there when he stayed over. A twinge of remorse settled in when Serena included an Armani suit jacket in the pile. But the remorse only lasted a second, replaced by an evil little grin and a serves him right attitude. She thought about calling him to come get it or take it to him but decided against it. She didn't want to have any connection with him; it was better this way. She still couldn't understand how he had thrown their love away and never looked back. Had he realized the pain he'd caused her or did he even care?

Serena didn't want to dwell on Kevin, it only made her sad. Instead, she thought about Astoria. She did have to admit, the thought of moving there was exciting; it was where her new life would begin, and the excitement had nothing at all to do with the possibility of running into Cliff. He was the furthest thing from her mind. Well, maybe almost the furthest. If she didn't ever see him again it would be alright by her. Yeah right, keep telling yourself that, Serena thought.

She reviewed her task list, checked off all that was accomplished and put stars by her unfinished tasks. Serena still needed to meet with Nina and give her the good news about promoting her. She couldn't wait to see her reaction, she sure did deserve it. This called for reservations at a special restaurant with a bottle of bubbly to celebrate her new position. She hadn't mentioned her idea to her dad yet. He had insisted she take over the shop and it would be nearly impossible to try and manage both businesses. She would bring it up tomorrow at dinner, hoping he'd be open to the idea. Serena also wanted to invest some time Sunday, working on the apartment in Astoria. It needed a good cleaning, painting and the boxed supplies moved to storage. Maybe she should also look into finding an exorcist to rid the apartment of the evil spirit, ghost, alien or whatever it was. She couldn't believe she was thinking like this. She just hoped to be moved and settled into her new place by the end of the month with little or no complications, and she didn't intend on sharing her new home with an uninvited guest.

Serena was also overjoyed that Lucy had agreed to stay on working full-time until Serena was ready to take over. Then, when Serena was comfortable handling the store on her own, she'd like to stay on part time for awhile, if that was okay with her. Serena loved the idea. Lucy would be good company and at the same time, help her transition into her new role and adapt to her new responsibilities. Also, with her working part time, Serena wouldn't have to worry about hiring and training someone new.

It was getting late and Serena still needed to call her mom and see if she needed her to bring anything to dinner tomorrow. Tess had talked Tom into coming; she said she would make it up to him. Serena announced that she didn't need the details and left it there. She was looking forward to the family gathering, it had been awhile since they were all together. She was also hoping to find time to talk to her mom if she could keep her off the computer long enough. With that thought, Serena giggled and prepared for bed.

The rain welcomed Saturday morning. It was a good day to curl up with a good book and veg out or catch a chick flick on the Hallmark channel. But for Serena, there would be no way for her to squeeze in even a little down time until she was settled. Today more packing was in order; mostly the odds and ends were left. Her mom wanted her to bring a dessert so that was on her list, and laundry was a must, if she wanted any clean underwear. So there went most of her day.

Barley after four o'clock, Serena pulled into her parent's driveway. Nearing her childhood home, she felt a pang of sadness. She would no longer be living close to them. No more hop, skip and jump and you're there. Astoria wasn't really that far, but to Serena it might as well have been on the other side of the United States.

Serena's mom and dad were on the porch, relaxing on the sofa, enjoying a late-day cocktail. Alice greeted her with open arms and a loving hug. "What did you do with my parents?" Serena asked with a chuckle.

"Tess and her family are in the house and she gave strict rules that all computers are off limits, which includes cell phones, iPods, etc. So we came out here," Mike informed his daughter.

Alice bent down and whispered in Serena's ear, "Good thing you're here, your father and I are bored out of our wits. You think you could talk your sister into changing her mind?" Alice pleaded.

Serena looked at her mom lovingly, "Mom you know how Tess is when she makes up her mind, and I'm sorry but I am going to agree with her decision. Can't we just sit and visit this time and put everything else aside? Besides, I was hoping I could get some mother-daughter time later."

Even though Alice didn't want to agree she nodded her head anyway, threw an arm around Serena's shoulder and gave her a kiss on her cheek. "Okay, you win," she apprehensively replied, and walked in to join the rest of the family.

Serena sat down beside her dad and gave him a hug. She decided now would be a good time to discuss Nina's promotion. Here it goes! "Dad you got a moment? I have something I'd like to talk with you about."

Mike looked up at his daughter and giving her his full attention, he answered. "I'm all ears, what do you need, honey?"

Serena started pleading her case. "Well, you are aware that I am moving and will be taking over Books on the Corner, so most of my time will be wrapped up there for a while. I wanted to propose that we promote Nina from Office Assistant to Assistant Manager and let her take over my duties here. She is a very devoted employee, a good friend and has been with the company for over ten years. She is already familiar with the everyday responsibilities of running the company now, and what she doesn't know, I will teach her. So, what do you think?" Serena asked, hiding her crossed fingers behind her back as she waited for her dad's response.

Mike pondered the questions and after weighing all the pros and cons in his head, he gave her his answer. "I see that you've given this considerable thought, and I do trust you to make the best decisions. I was hoping by this time to be back to work and then I could be taking up some of the slack, not sure if that will ever happen." Mike cleared his throat and continued. "This job is going to be a big responsibility; she is going to have to be dependable and trainable. We have built a fine business and I wouldn't want anything to jeopardize our success or reputation. Nina is a good choice and I trust your judgment. I'll be there to support her like I did you. So, the answer to your question is yes, we can promote Nina."

Serena let out a long breath and uncrossed her fingers. She had to admit she had been a little nervous and by the way he had been talking, she didn't know if this was going to end in her favor. But it did. She threw her arms around him and kissed him lightly on his cheek. "Thank you Daddy, you rock!" Serena said, feeling both relieved and excited. "I won't let you down; Nina will make the best assistant manager. I can't wait to tell her, she is going to freak. I plan on surprising her with the news next week. So with that done, let's go see what trouble our family has gotten themselves into."

"Go ahead and go on in, I need to go check the chicken." Mike stated.

As Serena stepped through the door, she was almost trampled on by her nieces who came running towards her. "Look, Aunt Sena, Mom let us wear the new outfits you bought us, she said they were for special occasions," Stephanie gleamed.

Serena joined both the girls in a group hug. "You both look very beautiful," Serena said, reaching into her purse to find her cell phone. "Here let me get a picture of you both." Five shots later, she had a collection of serious, cute and goofy pictures to add to her collection.

Crissy pulled Serena down and whispered in her ear, "you'd better put your cell away before Mom sees it, or it's going to go in the jar until you leave."

Serena almost broke out laughing but she tried hard to keep a straight face. "Thanks for the heads up, you think my sister would punish me for taking pictures of her babies?" Serena asked.

Crissy gave her a perplexed look and replied, "She might, Mom took Dad's and he was only checking the weather. We can't even play a video game!" She whined, with a pouty frown.

Boy, Tess was really taking this seriously, not going to be on the favorite-persons list tonight, that's for sure. Serena slid her phone into her purse and went to find the wicked witch of the west.

Serena found Tess in the kitchen preparing her favorite potato salad. She walked over to give her a hug. "See you're not making many points with the family tonight, are you Sis?" Serena teased.

"Well, somebody needed to take control of the situation before it got out of hand." Tess answered with a touch of sarcasm in her voice.

"I do agree, but better you than me." Serena said.

"I love you too!" Tess commented followed by a fake

smile. "I'll probably remove the curfew when everyone gets bored with one another or Mom starts throwing eye daggers my way." Tess laughed and then stepped back and took Serena's hands in hers. "Wow, looking good Sister, I like your new outfit. Next time I'll send you the memo too." Tess smiled as she embraced her sister in a hug.

"Thanks Tess, It's a little out of my comfort zone but I am starting to like the new look. It's going to take some time and we will probably have to go shopping again." Serena grinned.

"Such a hardship but I'll try and force myself to go with you." Tess teased, with a southern drawl, fanning her face with an imaginary fan. This caused them both to giggle.

"Where's Mom?" Serena asked. "I want to talk with her for a few."

"I think she's out on the back porch setting the table," answered Tess.

Serena excused herself and went out to the porch. She opened the French doors onto the patio, designed by her dad, but it had a few of her mom's womanly touches. The partially shaded stained deck that housed the outdoor kitchen would rival those of many master chefs. Her dad enjoyed cooking as long as it was outdoors. He was in his element out there; whether it was grilling a steak, roasting a chicken or firing a pizza in the outdoor oven. Occasionally he would tease her mom by saying "Now this is real cooking." Her mom would just smile and let him bask in his moment of glory.

Serena found her mom in the outdoor pantry looking for all the summer tableware and accessories. "Can I help you find anything?" Serena asked.

Alice looked up as Serena walked in. "Thanks, I'm just about done in here but you can set the table for me. Your dad is on the lower deck putting the last glaze on his barbecue chicken; then we should be about ready to eat in about fifteen minutes. What did you want to talk to me about honey?" Alice lovingly asked her daughter.

"Can we sit down for a minute?" A troubled Serena asked. "I haven't told you the entire story with Kevin and me," Serena started.

"Sure honey, just give me a couple minutes. I need to check on something in the oven and then we can talk for a bit." Alice said, while unloading the basket she had in her arms, before heading into the house.

"Okay," Serena said, taking the items out of the basket and setting the table. Even though the patio was built with a modern flair, the table in the center of the deck was the one thing that had never changed over the years. The family size round table with a lazy Susan top was custom built by her grandpa and dad many years ago. The table, painted in fun rainbow colors with matching chairs, made it an adventure at meal time and was a delight for all that came to dinner.

After setting the table, Serena walked over to the edge of the desk. She breathed in the sweet scent of her mom's honeysuckle plant as she took in the spectacular view of her parents landscaped tri-level yard. As children, she and Tess had spent many hours here creating a fantasy world.

The lush dark green grass set off the color of the foundation. A brick sidewalk guided you through the yard and down to the lower courtyard, where it came to a stop in front of a charming little gazebo. The handcrafted structure of white lattice and stone was the focal point of the yard and was Serena's favorite. Purple Clematises defined the arched doorway, and the bright yellow flower boxes containing a recipe of contrasting flower gave character to the outside of the building. Inside held a little bistro table set, two comfy wicker chairs and more hanging flowering baskets. When the weather was nice, it was a quiet and tranquil spot to enjoy a morning coffee, cozy up in the afternoon with a good book or just relax with a cocktail and take in the warmth of the late afternoon sun. The recessed lighting strung carefree around the outside gave way to a perfect setting for a romantic evening wedding. It was where Tess and Tom had exchanged their vows, and it was where Serena had also dreamed of marrying Kevin. She was still having a hard time accepting the fact that Kevin was not in her future, and wondered when memories of her broken dreams would stop haunting her. Pushing the thought of him out of her mind temporarily, Serena put her focus back on the scenery.

She loved the cement fountain that was centered in her mom's rose garden sanctuary. The dancing water brought life and motion to the middle courtyard. Crissy and Stephanie got enjoyment tossing coins into the pool and making wishes. Serena as a child would sit in the nearby swing and take in the fragrant scent of the roses, while listening to the sound of water music, offered by the fountain. Sitting on the opposite side of the fountain was a darling little pink playhouse, which her dad had designed and built for his girls when they were quite young. Her mom had picked out the furniture and decorated the inside. It was a special place, and she and Tess called it their secret hideout. Now it was a special place for her nieces.

Serena heard her mom calling which brought Serena back to the present. They sat down at the table as Serena prepared to pour her heart out to her mom.

Alice put her hand on Serena's to offer support. "I was sorry to hear about your breakup, your dad talked briefly about it with me. I figured you'd tell me the details when you were ready."

Serena gave a big sigh and began. "Well, that morning he wasn't making any sense. He kept talking a lot of nonsense. I have to admit I was very confused at first, especially since it was early and I hadn't had my coffee yet. Long story short, he hinted that our relationship was boring and he needed more excitement in his life. Unknown to me, he had already found miss excitement. I got the unwanted pleasure of seeing them together when I was out with Nina and it really hurt. Seeing them as a couple helped sway my decision to move to Astoria. It still feels so surreal. Serena admitted. "Am I ever going to be able to trust someone with my heart again?" Serena asked her mom.

Alice gave a loving smile and answered her heartbroken daughter. "Sure you will honey, it's just going to take some time." You will be on red alert for a while and it's going to have to be a special person to break that wall. I believe in time you will find each other."

Serena looked away from her mom to process her last statement, then staring down at her hands, she stated. "It was obvious that we weren't meant for each other," said Serena. "Do you believe there is a special someone for everyone in the universe, like a soul mate?" Serena asked, looking back at her for an answer.

"Yes, I do," stated Alice, taking Serena's hands in hers. Then she looked up and thought back in time. "It was love at first sight when I met your father, and with a lot of give and take on both sides, we built a strong and binding love for each other. It has even grown stronger since he had his stroke and realizing I could've lost him. We may fight and quarrel at times, but he is my best friend for life. In time, you will also find that special someone."

Serena's thoughts suddenly jumped to her encounters with Cliff. Was it possible he could be that special person? No, no, no; girl you are not going there, Serena chanted to herself.

Serena turned to her mom, gave her a big hug and said, "I love you Mom and someday I hope to have a relationship like you and Dad have."

Alice returned the hug and tenderly cupped her hands around Serena's face. She gently tucked Serena's hair behind her ears exposing her saddened eyes. She kissed her cheek and smiled. "I have faith you will honey, just be patient. By the way, I know this might be too soon, but you know my friend Barb, well her son is coming home to visit in a couple weeks and..."

Serena quickly interrupted, "Mom, I know where you're going with this, and you mean well, but I am not ready to date yet. I need some time to get my life back on track so, for now, I am going to put it in the hands of fate." *How was that working for her so far?* A quiet thought bubble popped into her head. She shrugged it off and placed a kiss on her mother's cheek. "Love you Mom, let's get the food on the table. I'm starved."

The dinner gathering was pleasant and uneventful and, they even found enough to talk about. They did find that life could go on without technology. After desert, Tess released the curfew, and even Serena was happy to find some quiet time to check some emails and take some group shots of the family. Serena excused herself early; she wanted to leave for the coast by seven the next day. She said her goodbyes, trying not to get over emotional as she thought about her move. It had turned out to be a good evening even if the wicked witch was there. Serena smiled to herself. Bless Tess's heart.

6) SERENA'S NEW HOME

The next morning, Serena was awarded with a welcoming clear blue sky and burst of sun. Even though it didn't bring with it warmth, it was a perfect day for a Sunday drive. She treated herself to a mocha and a muffin and prepared for the little trip. She loved to drive; it was a time to check in with her thoughts and see where they were at. At the present moment, they were flying off the board. She hoped the drive would help her to arrange them in a logical order or at least corral them into one place.

On her drive to Astoria, Serena was able to quiet her mind long enough to regroup and categorize her tasks in order of significance. The best way she found to accomplish that was to deal with first things first. Being the apartment was the highest priority, she would begin there. Serena had decided to clean today and come back during the week to paint. She had brought some cleaning supplies from home, and after a couple stops on her way, she would be ready to tackle that task. Next on her list was to finish packing up the odds and ends; most everything else was in boxes and waiting to be moved, unpacked, and placed in their new place. She had called to have the utilities transferred and scheduled for cable hookup. It wouldn't be too long before her little apartment was ready for her to move into.

Still, the thought of it becoming her new residence was a little daunting to Serena. She trusted her mind was leading her in the right direction; she only hoped that her heart would soon follow.

Walking into her soon-to-be new residence, Serena hugged herself and wondered if it would ever feel like her own. Maybe when all her belongings replaced the empty space, then it would seem more like home. Serena had a few things she needed to do before she could start cleaning. The two stops Serena had made on the way over were to collect supplies for a cleansing ritual, she hoped would rid the apartment of unwelcome spirits. The first was a little community church where she filled a tube with holy water, then to a veggie stand she found along the highway, for some garlic and sage. It might have seemed a bit silly, but she had no other ideas on how to scare off the strange presence that kept talking to her.

Serena went to each room leaving a clove of garlic and sprinkling drops of the holy water; fanning the smoke from a lit stick of sage completed the ceremony. Hopefully, this would do the trick Serena prayed, or she had made her apartment smell like a greasy kitchen diner for nothing.

"Lady," a voice spoke, startling Serena causing her to almost loose grip of the lighted sage. "I am not a vampire or an evil spirit, not sure what I am but I am pretty sure I can't hurt you."

Wow, Serena thought, this force was stronger than she'd imagined. Maybe she should've added a chant or did more research on exorcism. It was obvious her little ritual didn't have an impact on the spirit. What was she going to do now? She pondered. She could either meet this entity one on one or quickly leave the apartment, which her shaking legs were all for. Even though the thought of reaching out terrified her, Serena wasn't going to let the entity intimidate her. So finding her courage, she spoke slowly and clearly to the voice. "My name is Serena and I come in peace."

"Lady, or can I call you Serena? You can probably cross alien off your list as well," the voice announced.

"Then who or what are you?" Serena asked nervously, then added, "Serena is fine,"

"I am afraid that's a question I can't answer. I think I have been here for many years. I've tried talking to everyone that has come near the book, and you seem to be the only one that has been able to hear me," the voice admitted.

Looking around the room, Serena tried to follow the direction the voice was coming from. It led her to a closet where she opened the door and asked the voice to speak again. She traced it to a box buried in the far back corner. Inside the box was a book titled 'Trust, Honor and Obey.' What a funny name for a book she thought, picking it up and sitting on her cleaning stool.

As Serena opened the book, an old piece of yellowed paper slipped out. With shaking hands, she picked up the paper and said out loud. "A note fell out of the book. The print is pretty faded but I'm going to attempt to read it to you."

"'Here is James Hallow whom my heart did follow, we were engaged to be married and one day he did stray. It brought me much pain and I vowed to never be hurt me again. My heart it lays shallow and still, if I can't have him no other one will. In this book contains his spirit where he will remain until the day, he helps two lost souls find their way. Only one person can hear his plea and together they must discover the magical keys which will open the passage and set him free.' Oh, it also says at the bottom of the page in bold print; **this book is forbidden to leave the bookstore unless James is united with himself.**"

"What do you think this means?" Serena asked staring down at the old letter. "Do you think you could be James?"

"I guess it's possible, don't remember much. It sounds like you are supposed to help me though," the voice answered.

Serena put the book down and stepped back. "Oh no, that is never going to happen," Serena said with a shocked look on her face, slowly backing away from the book as if it were a live reptile. "I am not helping you or any other trapped soul. My life is just starting to get back on track and helping you was not on the list of getting there. I am truly sorry, but I just can't go there right now."

"Serena," the voice pleaded. "Please, you have to help me. I need to know who I am, how I got here and how to get out of this book forever. I beg of you."

"Could you at least tell me where I am?" The voice asked.

Serena didn't really want to add anything else to her already dysfunctional life. She did, however, feel a little sorry for the spirit. Maybe she could do some research in her spare time. She would only agree to help under her own terms. Serena couldn't believe she was about to bargain with a spirit. But if she didn't make an effort to help him, he would remain in this store and be a nuisance. She took a deep breath, let it out slowly and told him her decision. "Okay I will do it under the condition, that I work on my time and you only help when I ask. Is that agreed?"

"Agreed," said the appreciative voice.

"That settled, I am going to call you James for now. You are in my bookstore 'Books on the Corner' that used to belong to my departed Aunt Caroline. You reside in a hardcover book titled 'Trust, Honor and Obey' and that is all I know at this time. Does any of that ring a bell?"

The room went quiet, and then James spoke again, "I'm sorry to say, it doesn't. If only I could remember, maybe that would help put a piece in the puzzle. I don't understand why I am surrounded by all these words. I have scanned through this book from beginning to end and the words never change. It's like seeing a play over and over and over. What could I have done to have warranted such a punishment. Who or what put me in here?"

"I don't know the answers, but as soon as I get situated and my affairs in order, I'll find time to research. Right now, I have an apartment to clean."

For the next few hours, Serena focused on cleaning while rocking out to her favorite tunes. She had accomplished most everything on her list and all that was left was to move boxes and paint. She would put the boxes in the hall and sweet-talk her brother-in-law into taking them to storage. She said goodbye to James and was ready for the trip home. It had been a long and strange day. All Serena wanted to do was get back to Portland, grab a bite to eat and get some sleep. If her thoughts were reeling on her drive over, that was nothing compared to on her way back. Too much for Serena to grasp so she let her music drown them out. She would check in with them again at a later date. One thing for sure, it was going to be her secret. Who would believe her anyway? She thought.

Moving Day:

Sitting in her coffee shop waiting for her brother-in-law to arrive with her belongings, Serena was enjoying a freshly brewed espresso casting thought to the last week's events. Lucy, bless her soul had offered to paint the apartment which gave her more time to put all her affairs in order in Portland. Serena met Nina at the Grotto for dinner and celebration. When she told her about the promotion, Nina got so excited that Serena wondered if her happy dance would last all night. Serena had to admit she was just as excited for her friend. Nina had worked hard and deserved it. Even though Serena trusted that Nina was more than capable to take on her current responsibilities, there were still some matters Serena wanted to discuss with her. They agreed to meet again as soon as Serena was more settled in Astoria. For the time being, she would be coming into the corporate office on Thursday's and was only a phone call away, if Nina needed her. Serena's dad would also be available in case of emergencies. They toasted to Serena's new endeavors and Nina's promotion, they gave hugs and said their goodbyes, and with teary eyes, parted ways. Serena was really going to miss working with Nina.

A knock at the front door startled Serena out of her deep thoughts. She wondered why Tom hadn't walk in; the door was unlocked. A look of shock appeared on her face when she opened the door to find Cliff standing there. He looked so sexy in his tight blue jeans and flannel. Especially with his sleeves rolled-up, giving special attention to his muscular biceps. Serena was sure the temperature in the store had climbed twenty degrees. Thankfully the arrival of Tom and Tess interrupted the uncomfortable moment and brought Serena back to her senses.

Serena was the first to break the silence. "You must be the friend Tom was talking about."

"And you must be Tom's sister-in-law. It's a pleasure to meet you standing upright." He said with a teasing smile offering her his hand. Serena blushed and gave him a partial smile, shook his hand lightly and quickly let it go as if it was a poisonous snake.

Tom looked at Serena and back to Cliff. "You two know each other?" He asked, with curiosity plaguing his mind. Cliff looked at his friend. "Yes, this young lady has fallen for me twice, literally." Cliff laughed.

Serena didn't know why, but she was starting to get irritated with Cliff's sarcasm. She was afraid his teasing would get misinterpreted. She didn't want Tom and Tess to get the wrong idea.

Glaring at Cliff, Serena replied, "Yes we have met. I fell outside the store and then again on the beach and Cliff just happened to be there both times. If I remember correctly, the second time I had help by your trusty companion." Serena snapped, with sharpness in her tone, showing Cliff her looks-to-kill grin. Looking at Tom she emphasized, "We hardly know each other, barely acquaintances."

Cliff, a little offended by Serena's cold attitude, stared at the redheaded ice-princess and stated with a stern tone. "I told you I was sorry about the mishap on the beach and agreed to pay for your damaged items. I thought we were squared away." Then looking at Tom, Cliff strongly enforced. "She is definitely right we are just acquaintances, nothing more," Cliff added, taking on some of the sharpness himself.

Serena didn't know why she was letting this man get under her skin, but at this moment, she didn't care for his attitude. She started to reply but gave it a second thought. She didn't want to cause a scene in front of Tess and Tom so instead, she folded her arms, turned her head and pretended to ignore him.

Tom stood there witnessing their heated discussion and wondered if there was more to this story than what they were letting on. At any means, he needed to take hold of the situation, there was work to be done and he didn't plan on listening to these two bicker all morning. "You two sound like an old married couple, you can hash this out later on your own time. Right now, there is a full truck that needs unloading. So, if it's okay with you, I'd like to get started." With that said, Tom headed for the truck.

"Well let's get busy then!" Cliff commented glad to have the distraction as he followed Tom in that direction.

Now alone with her sister, Tess nudged Serena. "What's up with you and tall, dark and dreamy?" She asked with playful actions of fanning herself and batting her eyes. "

"What are you talking about? Serena said shrugging her shoulders. But noticing the look on Tess's face, Serena realized she wasn't buying her story and knew Tess would keep poking at her until Serena gave in. So she answered her question making sure to keep it brief. "Okay if you must know, he was the man who rescued me when I nearly fell in front of the shop the first night we were there. Don't get me wrong, I'm very grateful he was there. But there is definitely nothing between us or will there ever be," Serena emphasized, hoping her sister believed her better than she believed herself. She also didn't mention the beach scene because Tess would want all the details and Serena didn't want to go there.

"Well, you sure could've fooled me. I felt the chemistry the moment I walked into the room, and I saw the way his eyes were staring at you, Tess commented, following Serena into the coffee shop.

"You are delirious Tess." Serena said, pouring them both a cup of coffee. "We were both surprised to see each other again, that's all it was. He's not interested in me any more than I am in him besides, I am not looking for a new relationship," Serena said, attempting to plead her case.

Tess joined Serena at the table, not ready to drop the subject yet. "He seems very nice, and don't tell me you haven't noticed how good looking he is."

"Of course, I've noticed, I'm not blind, but a guy like that could only invite trouble and I'm not excepting that invitation." Serena said, shaking her head.

"I know you're not looking for anybody long term but maybe you could go out with him, have some fun with no strings attached," Tess commented, hoping she wasn't stepping over her sister's boundaries.

With her hands on her hips and an eyebrow raised, Serena remarked. "This suggestion is coming from my sister who wanted to wait until her wedding night?"

"Dear sister, I didn't mean you had to sleep with him, just go out and have fun," Tess continued. "I just want you to be happy and not feel so alone." Tess expressed, trying to hide the pain she was feeling about the move. "I won't be right down the street from you anymore. Who's going to look after you?" Tess stated with a hint of sadness in her voice.

Serena, after picking up their empty cups and putting them in the sink turned to her sweet sister. How had she'd been so blind to not see how this move was also hurting her sister. "Tess I am happy, and you're not that far away. I will be so busy learning about the bookstore that I won't have time to be lonely" (*and I have a spirit trapped in a book upstairs to keep me company),* A thought bubble appearing in her head. "*I* am going to call Rosie and see about getting together with her in the next week or two, and Lucy and I have lots of catching up to do. So how could I possibly have time to be lonely? I promise I'll try and call you every evening if I can." Don't worry I'll be just fine," Serena said to her sister, embracing her in a loving hug, hoping to put her fears to rest. "Now can we drop this subject and get upstairs? The guys are not going to know where to put things so we need to be there to direct them. It is also our prerogative to change our minds as many times as seen needed." That brought on a round of laughter as they headed up the stairs.

Cliff was glad that Tom had diffused the conversation. He couldn't believe he'd let that woman get under his skin. Why did she irritate him so much and at the same time spark his interest. Maybe he should get his head examined. Even though he knew he should forget about her, he found himself wanting to know more about her. He was hoping Tom could feed his curiosity. "Hey Tom, what's up with Serena? What's her story?" Cliff asked his friend.

Tom stopped what he has doing and paused for a second, then turning to face his friend, he answered. "She was engaged to Kevin, a man she met over three years ago; in fact, they were planning on getting married next spring. One morning, out of the blue, he told her that he wanted out of the relationship; it wasn't working for him anymore. It turned out the jerk had been cheating on her for a while.

It was quite a surprise to Serena, she hadn't seen it coming. As far as she knew, everything was fine. I have to tell you," stated Tom, noticing he was getting a little tense, he released his closed up fists. "When I heard the news, it took all my self-control and the threat from my dear wife to keep from giving him a surprise visit. She informed she would take the kids and go to her parents if I even thought about causing him harm. Even though she did agree he deserved it; she said Karma would get him someday. All I can say is that guy is lucky he is able to walk and he had better pray that I don't catch him alone someday. Anyway," continued Tom after taking a deep breath to calm down. "Serena was very hurt; it shook up her world big time. It's only been a little over a month, so if she seems a little sharp or short at times, it's because of everything she has been through. Usually she is a fun person to be around, a little on the crazy side at times, but she has a loving soul. In time, I'm sure she'll find her way back to that place."

Hearing what Tom had said brought a sudden flare of anger up to the surface for Cliff. Uncontrollable thoughts raced through his mind. The idea of someone being so cruel and insensitive to that little redhead, made Cliff want to find this Kevin guy and introduce his fist to his face, more than once. Where had that come from, he wondered? It wasn't like him to be a violent man but for some strange reason, he found himself wanting to protect Serena.

Tom stared directly at Cliff and with serious tone in his voice he warned his friend in a roundabout way. "If anyone hurts her again, they are going to have to answer to me and this time they won't be so lucky. I carry a soft spot in my heart for Serena. I love her like a sister."

Cliff stepped back waving his hands in front of him, knowing that some of that was directed at him, he needed to set Tom straight. "Whoa man, I am not interested in Serena; I do admit that she is intriguing but no more relationships for me for a while. Just left a bad one myself and not looking to jump into another. (*Even if she is a sexy little redhead*). Now put away your gun papa bear, and let's get this truck unloaded so we can grab a beer or two, we've got some catching up to do."

Tom patted his friend on the back "I am glad we have that settled, it makes me feel more at ease to ask this favor of you."

With a look of curiosity playing on his face, Cliff commented. "What's that?"

"Well, Tess and I were wondering if you would check in on Serena from time to time just to make sure she's okay. It would be a relief to know that someone is watching out for her, Tess especially would appreciate it. "

Cliff was surprised at what Tom was asking him to do and was taken aback by the request. "You want me to be her bodyguard?" A baffled Cliff asked.

Tom smiled at his friend. "No nothing like that. Just look in on her occasionally. Maybe when you're in the neighborhood, you could stop in at the shop and see how she is."

He was honored that his friend put so much trust in him, but he wasn't sure he could trust himself around Serena. Cliff did understand Tom's concern and he supposed it wouldn't hurt him to drop in once in a while and see how she is doing. It wasn't like he had to be with her night and day. Even though it was against his better judgment, he decided to help out his friend out. "Guess I could do that. I'm going to be working on the jewelry store up the street, they want to enlarge their shop, so I won't be far away."

"Thanks a lot, man," Tom said with a sigh of relief, patting his friend on his back. You don't know how much this means to us. Please don't mention our little talk to Serena; I am afraid she wouldn't be all that happy with you or me. Let's just keep this our little secret, okay?" Tom stressed.

"Sure man, you can count on me," Cliff answered. He still wasn't sure this decision was in his best interest, but he had made a deal with Tom and he never pulled back on his word. With that said, the men started the grueling job of unloading the truck.

The morning went pretty smooth. While Serena and Tess spent the morning unpacking and organizing Serena's things, the guys unloaded the truck, and were very patient with the girls, as they kept changing their mind on the placement of the furniture. Cliff and Serena avoided each other like the plague, as much as they could in such a small area. She was polite to him and vice versa and they talked to one another only when necessary. He made her uncomfortable, so she tried to keep her distance. She was grateful her sister and Tom were there since she wasn't sure she could trust her own actions. Serena planned on keeping her heart as many beats away from Cliff as possible.

By two o'clock, Serena's stomach reminded her that she hadn't eaten lunch. She imagined the rest of the crew were also getting hungry, and decided to take them all out for lunch. They had all worked hard and they deserved it. "Hey guys, who wants to go grab a bite somewhere?" Serena asked the group. "It's my treat." She added.

Grinning, Tom leaned his arm on the dolly and offered his suggestion. "In that case, I want steak and lobster."

Serena returned the comment with a quirky smile, "Yeah right! Nice try brother. Do I hear any other reasonable suggestions?" Serena giggled.

"I could go for a good hamburger and a diet coke," Tess voted.

"That sounds perfect to me also," Serena agreed.

Serena looked up at Cliff who happened to be watching her. This made her feel uneasy and for the life of her she couldn't figure out why. He had been a tremendous help, and even though he got on her nerves, she didn't want to be rude and exclude him. What harm could it be? It was just lunch, not a date.

"Cliff." Serena said, trying not to sound too nervous. "Since you know this area, can you suggest a place that will make us all happy? You are also welcome to join us. If it wasn't for your help with the heavy items, Tess and I would have had to help Tom lug them up the stairs and it wouldn't have been a pretty picture. So the least I can do is treat you to lunch. Tell me where and I will let the Garmin lead us there." Serena said, tucking an escaped hair from her ponytail behind her ear.

Cliff wasn't sure going to lunch with her was a smart idea, his emotions were going sideways and being around the hot little mess would only make them worse. To top it off his hormones were in full gear and his senses were not engaging on all cylinders either. He needed to be careful and safeguard his heart. However, it was just lunch and he was hungry, besides Tess and Tom would be there. It's not like it was a date, he thought.

They ended up at a little restaurant not far from her shop. Tom had found his steak and the rest ordered a burger. Cokes for the ladies and the guys opted for a Bud. Serena thought to herself, it had been a good day. She was now moved in, just needed to finish unpacking and do some rearranging, but there would be lots of time for that. She took a quick peek at the sexy man across from her, he had been a big help and nice to her most of the time. His sarcastic remarks had hit Serena the wrong way and she, herself, had been caught off guard, causing her to be a little sharp with him. Not one of her better moments, that's for sure. She would have to apologize for her actions, it was uncalled for. Who knows maybe they could just be friends. She would have to think on that and find out if her mind and heart were okay with that decision.

She looked around her table; everyone was eating, talking and laughing. They looked so relaxed, enjoying their time together. Serena felt a sense of calming warmth and security, something she hadn't let herself feel for a while. She sat in a serene state of mind taking in these beautiful moments.

Cliff watched Serena; he had to admit he liked this side of her. She was so beautiful and those jeans and sweater hugged her just enough to show off those hidden curves. She seemed so much more relaxed. It was probably because she felt secure with Tess and Tom around. He was getting a glimpse of the softer side of her and for some reason it scared him half to death. So much different than the snobby uptight girl he had first met. He couldn't blame her though for putting her guard up. At least he hadn't been engaged to Tandy. He was lucky he hadn't let their relationship get that far.

After lunch, Serena took everyone back to the shop. They had the rest of the truck unloaded and most of the furniture in their temporary spaces within the next hour. Task done, they said their goodbyes. Cliff had to leave, Brody needed out, fed and walked. Tess and Tom wanted to head back, they still needed to pick up the girls and get a movie. Tonight was family night. Serena felt a little pang of jealousy as she watched Tess and Tom walk out arm in arm. She had longed for the relationship and family that her sister had. Someday, Serena someday, she chanted. But for now, she needed to find the balance in her new life before she could think of love and a family.

It had been a long day and Serena was looking forward to a little downtime. She planned on toasting herself with a glass of Chablis as she got acclimated to her new place. At least she wouldn't be there by herself. She laughed at her thought. She wondered how Tess would've reacted if she had told her not to worry, she wouldn't be alone because she was sharing it with a spirit in a book. She would've said she was crazy, demanded to stay the night and make Serena go home with her the next day. Serena would have to find just the right time to spring the news on her. Or not.

"Hello," Serena greeted James as she entered the apartment. "Thank you for being quiet." Serena added as she stared down at the book as if it were real. She had made a deal with him, if he promised to be quiet during the move, then she would start researching. He had kept his end of the bargain and even though Serena was exhausted, she would spend a little time helping him.

"I told you that you are the only one that can hear me so I don't know why I had to be quiet?" James asked.

"I know, but it would have been distracting and awkward." Serena commented. "It still baffles me that I am the only one that can hear you," She added.

James hesitated for a moment and spoke, "That's also a mystery to me; believe me, I've tried many times. Maybe you have some connection to the spirit world."

Serena pondered that statement and shook her head. She just couldn't accept the possibility. It was totally out of her realm of reality. "It's probably a one-time spiritual connection. I'm pretty sure my calling wasn't to be a ghost whisperer."

Serena's remark caused James to laugh. "Oh well, I wouldn't worry about it now Serena but there is something I am wondering about." James said, pausing for a second. "From what I could gather, Tess is your sister and Tom is her husband so where does this Cliff fellow fit in? Is he your boyfriend?" James asked.

Serena chuckled and responded waving her hands in front of her. "Heavens no, he's an old friend of Toms, he asked him to help unload the truck. He's okay, I guess."

"You may say that Serena, but I don't think you're being quite honest with yourself. There is much more there than you see; I could sense a strong connection between you two. I felt it with Tess and Tom. It must be because of my spiritual awareness. With your sister and husband, I sensed the presence of two powerful beings that are bonded together into one. With Cliff and you it was much different, like two electrical currents leaving sparks in their wake." James admitted.

"Argh," Serena commented in frustration as she pushed her hair out of her eyes. "Why does everyone think something is going on between us? He is a nice guy but I barely know him. You must be mistaken. Maybe your connection has its signals crossed."

"I guess it's possible," James replied, " but I don't think so. It seemed to get stronger the closer you two got to one another."

"You see James," Serena stated. "This can't happen, I don't want any type of connection with this man or any other man right now, spiritual, physical or mentally. I can't go there. It would be a careless move and prove to be dangerous."

"Serena I don't understand why you are so afraid of him. Something is pulling you two together, but there seems to be a resistance on both ends, when it's obvious you are perfect for one another. Maybe you both have trust issues. There is a chapter in this book on that very subject; it might be worth reading sometime," James offered.

Serena couldn't believe she was getting advice on trust from a book. What was next, the cookbooks were going to start giving her cooking lessons? She couldn't see how her life could get any stranger.

Oh but it will, James thought to himself.

"Hey, Serena. Do you think it's possible that you are the one I'm supposed to help?" James asked, as he remembered the words in the letter she had read to him.

Noooo! Serena screamed in her mind. It couldn't be her. She didn't need help finding anyone. This was a time-out period for her, and when she was ready Mr. Right would appear. "James, don't be ridiculous," Serena answered with a slightly hysterical laughter. "Why would you think that? I certainly don't need any help finding anyone, but someone does and we need to find out who that person is!" Serena exclaimed, driving the conversation away from her. "I'm not sure yet how we are supposed to accomplish that. I guess the best place to start is by searching the Web," Serena announced. "It's going to take me a few minutes to get my computer hooked up then we can Google your name and see what we can find out about you."

James wasn't sure what strange language Serena was talking in; he had never heard the terms Web, or Google. It was obvious that he had missed a lot being trapped in the book for many years.

After setting up the computer and pouring herself a glass a wine, Serena figuratively put on her detective hat and said to the entity, "first, let's search on your name; James Hallow." "Hmm," Serena mumbled, as she studied the list that appeared on her screen, nervously tapping the pencil on the desk. "There are twenty hits on your name in this surrounding area. First we need to eliminate the ones that don't apply, so I am making a list." Serena informed James thinking the name Hallow must have been a popular name back then.

James listened to Serena as she spewed out the computer lingo and tried to follow along the best he could.

Serena took some notes as she went down the list; "Four are under the age of twenty, three are married, six are dead, five are missing and two don't match the time frame. I presume you are either on the missing or dead list, so we'll start there," stated Serena. "Are you sure you can't remember names dates, events, anything that may help?"

Serena asked, as she sat staring at the book lying on the table as though she was talking to a real person.

"Believe me, if I could I'd tell you. Something may strike up an interest, let's keep going." James commented excited to continue the conquest that may lead to his road home.

"Okay, Serena said, putting her focus back on her list. Let's check the people on the missing list first. Hmm, I found one child who went missing when he was six but thankfully he was found. This one is strange, it's a dog. Who in their right frame of mind, would name their dog James Hallow? Unless you're reincarnated, we can rule that one out. Just to be sure," Serena snickered. "Let me hear you bark." She had to find some humor in this ludicrous situation she had found herself in. Not too many people were spending their Saturday nights on the computer, trying to find out the identity of a lost soul. She guessed she was one of the lucky ones.

"Very funny lady, I am pretty sure I am not part of the canine family, so let's proceed with me as human form shall we." James commented. He was intrigued with her sense of humor. It showed she was loosening up a bit. He knew this must be an awkward situation for her, and he was grateful to have her help. Hopefully, she would understand when he broke the other news to her later that night.

"So, kidding aside, here's one that may be promising." Serena said as she continued. "James Mathew Hallow, a well-known political figure in the community, disappears after a weekend convention at the Wellford Hotel. His disappearance baffled the police but after months of searching, he was added to the cold case files. Some speculated that it was foul play but nothing was ever proven."

"Think that may be you?" Serena asked James.

"It doesn't ring a bell, but at this point anything is possible. What if I can't remember anything about my past? How am I going to be of any help to you?" a distressed James asked.

Serena felt bad for James; it had to be rough on him not knowing his identity or history pertaining to his mortal life. Spending day after day just existing in a book was not much of a life, or would it be afterlife. She was destined to find out who and where he came from. In a way they were like two lost souls searching for something. James; a key to freedom and Serena; she wasn't quite sure. Hopefully she'd know when it was found.

Followed by a long stretch and yawn, a tired Serena stated, "James we just got started, there are still more on the list. Don't get discouraged, the internet is an amazing place to find out almost anything. We are bound to find something," Serena said, trying to reassure the spirit. "Tomorrow I'll check the rest on the list and tap into the Astoria Library. There are bound to be newspaper articles there with more information about James Mathew. That's all for tonight. I want to drink my wine, put my feet up and get lost in the view of the lights on the river."

"Thank you; I appreciate all your time and compassion. You

are a good person Serena. I didn't find out anything about me which is unfortunate, but I am interested in hearing about you. Could you also tell me about this web?" James asked, hoping that she would take him up on his offer. He sensed that there was so much hurt and sadness in that girl by the vibes she projected. What had caused it? James wondered.

Serena thought about the question. She felt a sense of peace and calmness around the spirit. He didn't pose a threat. It would be like talking to an invisible therapist. She could talk and talk and he couldn't go anywhere, Serena thought, as she smiled to herself. Here it goes; she would probably need a real therapist when this was over.

First Serena decided to keep it light as she gave James a brief training on computers 101 and Cell 101. It would've have been more effective with visuals;, hopefully, James was able to grasp the new technology, even if he probably wouldn't need it where he was destined to go. Then she opened up and expelled all her raw emotions. Serena found herself telling James all about her life. She reached down and exposed her inner fears, hopes and dreams. She talked about her childhood, schooling, wonderful parents, sister, and her dad's stroke. All the friends she had made and some she had lost. Serena even found herself divulging things her sister didn't know. The hardest part was when she opened up and shared about Kevin. She hadn't realized how much pain she was still in and how much resentment she was harboring. She was going to have to work on letting things go, so she could start to heal.

James listened without as much as a word. For the most

part, life had been good to Serena. It had its ups and downs and ebb and flows, no different than anyone else's. It had been temporarily turned upside down, but he had no doubt she would pull through. He wondered about his life. What was it like? There were so many questions and very little answers. James had no comments and left Serena with her thoughts.

Serena sat there welcoming the silence and became lost in her thoughts. She tried quieting her mind as she embraced the view of the beautiful lights, painting pictures on the water. Serena remained in that blissful state until she could no longer fight her tiredness. She prepared herself for the first night in her new bed and home, and hoped for a peaceful and restful night. There wasn't an explanation but Serena felt serenity and relief surrounding her as she drifted off to sleep.

Serena awoke that night to an eerie presence she felt in the room. She opened her eyes to find a faint shadow of a man, floating over her bed. She closed her eyes and spoke out loud to herself, "You are just overly tired, emotionally drained and you have a spirit living in your home, you're bound to have some strange dreams." Serena then heard a familiar voice speaking to her.

"You are not dreaming and don't be alarmed it's me James."

"Don't be silly, it's just my mind playing tricks on me. James you are in a book. Now I would appreciate it if my dream state would move along, I am very tired," Serena said in a sleepy voice, followed by a yawn. Then with a fluff of her pillow, she was down again.

"Serena it really is James, there's something you don't know about me. Please let me explain." The voice spoke again.

Serena opened one eye and noticed the shadow was still there. She opened the other, and tried to get all the gears working in her brain, at least enough to pull her out of the sleep-induced haze. Sitting up, she tried to focus, hoping that any minute she would awake from this nightmare. But to her surprise, the figure was still there. No matter how many times Serena opened and closed her eyes, she could not remove the image from her mind. It was really starting to freak her out, especially when it became clear to her that it wasn't a dream at all. That's when Serena heard a blood-curdling scream. It took her a few seconds to realize, it was coming from her.

7) A MIDNIGHT SIGHTING

James hadn't realized what an impact his changing form would have on Serena, but it was obvious it wasn't a pleasant one. He must look scarier than he thought. He needed to calm her down fast, before the neighbors started checking on the screams coming from a neurotic lady. One thing for certain, she sure had some powerful lungs on her. "Calm down Serena, take some deep breaths and listen to me. There is no reason to get alarmed."

Serena, who was fully awake now and trying to grasp what was going on, said with a stutter, "Who; who are you? How many of you are lurking in this apartment, ready to attack me when I am not looking? I am sure there must be more." Serena said, her eyes wide open and alert and scanning the room. Before the ghostly figure could explain, Serena had jumped out of bed, turned on all the lights and started frantically going through all her closets, drawers and cupboards, leaving a destructive wake in her path as she tossed things left and right.

"What in the world are you doing?" James asked as he tried to make sense of her behavior.

"What do you think I'm doing? Serena answered. I'm looking for the rest of you creatures." Not giving much thought on how her nerves would handle it if she did encounter anymore. "No wonder this apartment was vacant so long," Serena shrieked. "Who could live here without going crazy? There is a spirit trapped in a book and ghost-like entities visit you late in the night, all the comforts of home and a little more." Serena shrieked again in a high pitched tone, adding to the mess already in progress in her apartment. By this time, it was beginning to look like a tornado had blown through it.

James decided to just let Serena wear herself out, so he folded his arms and decided to watch the show. Sooner or later she would either break or slow down. He was hoping for the later. "Just let me know when you're finished." James announced to Serena.

After about fifteen more minutes, Serena finally threw herself down on the bed. The day had taken a toll on her, and added to the energy depleted by the shock, she felt deeply exhausted. She sat up, realizing what a mess she had made in her apartment, she gasped in horror. What had she done? Well if it wasn't a dream, then she had to come to the conclusion that it really was James. At this point, the impossible in her life was becoming the possible. So this is what her life had become. If she told anyone they would surely have her put away. She immediately grabbed the book and demanded that he return. "Get; get, back in this book where you belong, James! What are you doing out anyway?" Serena asked curiosity plaguing her mind.

"I can't go back in there now." James proceeded to explain, "The same spell that keeps me in the book pulls me out at midnight and pulls me back in before sunrise. It's very annoying," James alliterated.

"See, I knew it!" Serena shrieked again. "You are a vampire! You may not drink blood but you suck the souls out of innocent people while they are sleeping."

James sighed. "I thought we covered the fact that I'm not a vampire. I don't drink blood or steal souls, I just wander around the shop innocently night after night after night."

"I know, that's what you told me," an irritated Serena answered, raising her hands above her. "But that was before you appeared in your ghostly form. Don't you think, maybe, just maybe, it, might have been an important fact to share with me, instead of scaring me half to death in the middle of the night?"

"Probably" James answered. "I'm sorry I frightened you Serena, but I was afraid if you knew the truth, it would scare you off. You're my only hope of getting out of here. It was wrong, but desperation got the best of me. Please accept my deepest apology." James said, hoping that he hadn't ruined his only chance at freedom.

Serena couldn't believe she was having this discussion with an inhuman form. What did she ever do to deserve such a punishment? As surreal as it seemed, Serena needed to get a hold of the unfamiliar situation and try to make some sense of it. She needed to set some boundaries that would benefit both her and James and protect her sanity, if there was any left.

"James." Serena said calmly. "For now, let's table this discussion. It's late and I am beyond tired," she said while trying to relax. "One thing for sure, I can't have you in this room floating around, or whatever you do all night. So from now on, after midnight, unless I'm awake, you will not be allowed in this bedroom. I will make sure to put the book in the living room before I go to bed at night. Agreed?"

"Agreed," James said, so relieved that she wasn't going to give up.

"Hey James, I am curious about something. Are you able to see me, I mean all of me?" Serena asked, feeling very exposed, pulling the covers up to her neck.

"No, not in the way a human would see you. There is a blue energy force in the shape of a human that changes color depending on their mood. I can see you move and your actions but it is filtered. Right now you are a little black, which is understandable after your scare."

"So!" Serena giggled hysterically, "I look like a human mood ring."

"Yes, I guess something like that," James commented, not

sure what she was talking about. "What about me?" he asked.

Serena studied the ghostly form and answered, "I can see a very faint shadow of a man in a glowing form. That's all."

"I was hoping you would see more detail, something that might define who I am," James remarked, with a little sadness hidden in his voice.

"Nope, sorry, maybe someone more connected to the spirit world could see you better. I do have one more question to ask you." Serena said with a yawn, as she felt the night pulling her back down to rest.

"What is that?" James asked.

"Are there any more surprises you're not telling me about? Such as; you moan and groan, rattle chains or morph into gross creatures?"

"I promise, no more surprises," James answered. "I'll be as quiet as a mouse. I can't do much anyway. It's kind of hard in this form, and besides I can't see things in their current state. I will leave and let you get back to sleep. Good night and sweet dreams." On that note, Serena watched James slowly fade away as she drifted back to sleep.

The next morning, Mr. Headache was back. Lack of sleep and a night spirit sighting were a contributing factor for sure, a fuzzy-headed Serena thought to herself.

Everybody should have a night like that. Why should she get all the glory? She needed to keep light of the situation; if she fell too deep, she would lose grasp of reality. An aspirin, a banana, and some coffee, followed by a long run on the beach, should fix her right up. As she sat up realization hit her. The disaster in her apartment reminded her of the bizarre night she had. She'd just gotten everything put away and now it was all strung out in her apartment. "Arg," she spoke out loud, angry at herself for her temporary bout with insanity. This mess was going to take her a while to clean up, but it would just have to wait until she got back from her run.

Down by the waterfront, Serena did some light stretching before taking off on her run. She wasn't envisioning any surprises but just in case, she kept her volume low on her temporary head seat. Had she been hoping to see Cliff or Brody? She posed the question and decided either way was fine with her. Or was it? She thought.

After her run and more coffee, Serena was feeling better and ready to tackle her day. She was thankful it was only Sunday; at least she'd have one more day to adjust to her new surroundings. Serena wanted to familiarize herself with the layout of the store. She was in her element in the coffee shop but there was so much to learn in the bookstore.

She and James had shared some small talk before her run. Serena was getting used to having the entity around. As strange as it seemed, she didn't feel so alone having his presence there. She would, however, have to find a way to adjust to his changing form. That part still felt a little creepy to her. Most people had pets for companionship. She bet there weren't many people that had a spirit as a roommate. A dog would be so much easier. With that thought, she smiled and headed upstairs to deal with the mess and shower.

The apartment back together and Serena feeling better, she prepared herself for a long hot shower. But to her surprise, when turning off the faucet, she was greeted with a couple spurts of water and then nothing. Great! Serena thought. What was she going to do now? She settled for a quick sponge bath in the sink for the time being and then put a call into Lucy. Maybe she could recommend a plumber.

"Hi Luce," Serena greeted her cousin. "Hope I'm not catching you at a bad time?" Serena asked, hearing the twins yelling at one another in the background.

"No, I have a couple minutes then we're off to church, hold on a sec," Lucy said, moving the phone away from her mouth and calling to the twins. "Hey, you two quiet down, I'm on the phone." Temporary silence fell for a minute and then the boys were at it again. "Sorry about that. The boys are fighting; you know, brotherly love." She laughed and continued. "I am sorry I couldn't join you all down at the shop yesterday to help with the move, but something came up. I hope all went well." Lucy replied.

"Yes, it did and don't worry about not being there, I had plenty of help." Serena answered. "I'm all moved in and trying to get settled. Hey, Luce, I don't want to keep you too long, but the reason I called is because there isn't any water coming out of the shower. I was wondering if you might know of a plumber that may be willing to come to my rescue on a Sunday?" Serena asked.

"Hmm," Lucy said as she gave thought to Serena's questions and answered. "I do in fact; wait a minute I have his card on the fridge." Lucy informed Serena. After a brief pause, Lucy was back on the phone with the information. "Here it is," she said. "His name is Cliff Hallow, a local plumber and contractor, very efficient and reasonable. I've had to call him a couple times, and the bonus is he's quite handsome." Lucy emphasized, in the same breath apologizing for the loud interruption of the twin's outburst, while attempting to read off the phone number to Serena.

"Thanks, Lucy, you're a doll. See you tomorrow. Loves," Serena said.

"Loves to you too and good luck, hopefully, it's nothing big. Bye," Lucy said, ending the call.

Serena hung up the phone and went to find the business card that Cliff had given her. A look of shock appeared on her face as she read the card. "Cliff Hallow Licensed Plumber and Contractor. Great, same name and contact number." Serena added with a heavy sigh.

Well, she needed a plumber, and had no choice but to call him or go without a shower. That just wasn't happening. A sudden surge of excitement rang through her; maybe she would put on a little makeup, some perfume and get out of her running clothes. Not that she cared what she looked like when he got there, she was just feeling a little grungy that's all.

It took her a moment to realized, as she reread the card, that James and Cliff had the same last name. She wondered if it was just a coincidence, or was it possible they were related? Maybe when she was talking to Cliff about the shower, she could nonchalantly bring up the subject. .

Cliff was surprised to get the call from Serena. He wasn't doing much today except kicking back and watching a little sports on the tube, so he agreed to come over. He told himself that he was just going over there and see if he was able to fix her shower, then leave. He would treat it as though it was just another job, even though the customer was a hot little redheaded mess. One he was having a hard time getting out of his head.

Serena was enjoying a cup of coffee when Cliff arrived. He had brought Brody and after accepting a gentle rub from Serena, he made himself a comfy bed on the floor in the children's corner. "Hi," Serena said greeting Cliff with a friendly smile, taking in his looks and liking what she was seeing. "Thank you so much for coming over on a Sunday, I really appreciate it."

"No problem." Cliff admitted, also enjoying the view facing Serena. "Brody and I were just hanging out today; maybe head over to the beach later for an afternoon run, depending on the weather." Brody perked up when he heard the word beach. "Lay back down boy, we will see about that in a while." Cliff said, commanding his dog.

Serena smiled, taking in the camaraderie between man and dog. "He sure is a smart dog, and well mannered." She commented.

Cliff returned the smile and commented, "Yeah he's a pretty good dog most of the time that is when he isn't knocking down people on the beach." Cliff laughed. "I swear he knows what I'm saying, and he appears to also comprehend it. Believe me, sometimes it creeps me out."

Not as creepy as having a spirit living with you, a silent though-bubble appeared in Serena's head.

Serena, trying to get her mind back in focus, walked over and picked up the coffee pot. "Would you like a cup?" Hoping he would accept, so she could ask him about James.

Cliff gave a nod of thanks as he sat down at the table, "I don't need any of that foofy stuff in it, I just like it black."

"Right," Serena answered

Sitting down at the table, Serena looked up at the man across from her, it felt so natural being there with him. It seemed as though they had known each other longer than just a few days. She could get lost in those eyes and be smothered by his kisses and... What in the world was she thinking? Focus, Serena focus.

"Cliff, before we get started." Serena said, pausing to take a sip of her coffee, "I have a crazy question to ask you."

Cliff sat back in his chair, folded his arms in front of him and with a smile replied, "Ask away, what is it you want to know?"

Serena took a silent breath and thought to herself, here it goes. "Well, when I was going through some boxes of my aunts, I came across this letter that referenced a man by the name of James Hallow." Serena paused and took a sip of her coffee, she wasn't going to go into detail; he would probably think she was a nut case. She set down her cup and continued as she tried to read the expressions on his face. "I was just wondering if he might be related to you."

Cliff was caught off guard by the question. Of all the things she could've asked him, he never imagined it would be about his family. Cliff smiled, unfolded his arms and thought about how to answer her question. "I guess he could've been. My dad had five brothers. I met three of my uncles, and the other two left when my dad was still in high school. They took on lives that my grandpa didn't approve of. All my uncles have the word James in their name, my great granddad's name was James Scott Hallow and my granddad thought he would honor him by giving his name to all his sons." Cliff paused for a moment and set down his cup. "Let me see if I can get the names right." Cliff said, while searching through his memory files in his brain.

Serena listened and watched Cliff; she liked the way he scrunched up his forehead when he was deep in thought. She also noticed he hadn't shaved yet and the five o'clock shadow he was sporting was hot. Serena could've sworn that the heat index climbed fifty degrees in the last five minutes. It was probably just hormone overload. She needed to corral them before they broke out of the fence and went looking for trouble.

"Michael James Hallow," Cliff continued, bringing Serena back from her fantasy world. "My favorite uncle. He was a longshore fisherman and was out on the boat for weeks. I can still remember sitting around in the evening listening to all the stories and hanging on to every word. I was just a young boy back then, and I couldn't wait for his return from his journeys to hear more stories. Of course, they were embellished and the more he drank the wilder they became. Funny," Cliff thought leaning back in the chair to stretch his legs; "I haven't thought of Uncle Michael for many years. He died when I was 22, in a car accident; sure do miss him."

Serena studied Cliff and was touched by his sharing. Putting her hand on his arm to add comfort, she could immediately feel the electricity between them. She knew it was a big mistake but at the same time Serena didn't want to let go. "I am sorry to have caused you to bring up sad memories; that was never my intention. Your uncle did sound like a good man and I would have like to have known him."

Cliff , not sure how to respond to her touch was also aware of the energy flowing within and knew this probably was wrong, but her touch went deeper than just to his skin. He nonchalantly took her hand, gave it a little squeeze and told her that he was fine. He continued telling her about his uncles as he got up to refill his coffee cup. This made a good excuse to divert the direction he felt they were heading in.

"Now, where was I? Oh yeah, my Uncle Lester;   Lester James Hallow, I believe. Boy, was he a character. He worked in the mill nearby and his second home was the Corner Side Bar. I remember my Aunt Wanda always going down there to drag him home. I also believe he had some lady friends on the side. I can't remember too much about him except that when he was drinking, us kids would hit him up for money. Surprised that man never went broke." Cliff laughed. Then his face went solemn. "He died a few years back from alcohol poisoning, such a waste."

Serena saw the sadness in Cliff's eyes, but decided to be quiet while Cliff proceeded with his small snapshot of his life.

"Last, but not least, there is my Uncle James Thomas Hallow who is still alive and doing quite well. He invested in the internet and earned enough for an early retirement, which allows him and his wife to travel."   His base home is located in Southern California and he makes it up here every couple years. Come to think of it, they are just about due here in a couple months.   I don't know if that helped much. I'm sorry but I don't know much about the last two, they weren't around when I was growing up. I'll ask my dad, he should know. After all, they were his brothers."

Well, Serena thought, she could rule out all them except for vagabond uncles. She couldn't imagine James being a bad person, he seemed so nice and had a decent soul.

"Thank you. It wasn't important, I was just curious that's

all. I did enjoy hearing about your family and would like to hear more about them, but I don't want to keep you all day. Brody wouldn't be happy with me if he didn't get to go to the beach," Serena said, keeping her voice quiet so not to alert Brody. "Come on, let me show you the shower."

Cliff followed Serena up to her apartment. He especially liked the little bounce she had in her step. He had to admit he enjoyed spending the morning with her and was a little sad that he was only there to look at her shower. Probably for the best though, he could get use to that precious redhead and she could only bring him trouble. He was going to try and keep this visit strictly focused on business.

Serena led Cliff to a small door off the bedroom. With a small box in his hand, he crawled through a little passageway where he found the piped plumbing. After about fifteen minutes, he came out with a pipe that was all corroded inside. "Well," he said, handing the pipe to Serena. "No wonder you don't have any water, by the looks of it, I'd say it hasn't been used in quite some time."

"Eww," Serena said as she examined the pipe. "This doesn't look good. So what is your solution?"

"You want the good news or the bad news first?" Cliff asked, as he put his tools away.

"Go ahead and give me the bad first, I'm a big girl I can take it. Just don't tell me it's haunted."

Cliff gave Serena a strange look. "Why would you think that?"

"Never mind, it's not important." Serena said, trying to bypass the thought bubble she let escape.

"Anyway," Cliff continued, mentally pondering her last comment, and dismissing it. He was sure that there was still something she wasn't telling him. "The bad news is, you can't use your shower until I get a new pipe to replace this one. The good news is, I can get one tomorrow and have your shower working by the afternoon."

Serena let out a big sigh; she was hoping to have it fixed today and was so looking forward to a long hot shower. She handed the pipe back to Cliff with a disappointed expression on her face. "I was hoping to be able to use it today. What am I supposed to do for a shower? I can't wait until tomorrow," Serena whined, giving Cliff the sad-puppy-eyed look. "Is there a public shower in town?" She asked.

Cliff studied Serena, as she stood only inches from him. He wondered what it would be like to take her in his arms and kiss those pouting lips, but as he started to move closer, Serena was startled by an awful sound which caused her to scream and jump back. She wasn't positive, but she had a suspicion it had come from James.

A stunned Cliff was trying to figure out what had just happened as he stared at Serena in bewilderment.

Thinking fast Serena plotted a story. "Sorry about that I thought I saw a spider over there in the corner" Serena pointed.

Cliff walked over to the direction to check out her story. "There doesn't seem to be a spider there now. You must have scared him off, and probably all the spiders in a fifty-mile radius," laughed Cliff.

Whew, she fixed that one. She would talk with James later about his sudden outburst. "So, is there a public shower?" Serena repeated.

"Serena, I don't have a clue, never had the need for one. There is a perfectly good shower at my house and you're welcome to use it."

As intriguing as it sounded, the shower of course, Serena didn't think it was a good idea. She was becoming way too dependent on this man, and too comfortable around him. All these emotions were swimming inside her and she didn't know if she could control them or herself. There was something that almost happened between them right before James's interruption. She could feel it, and it probably wouldn't be a smart idea going to his house. "Thanks but I have already taken up most of your morning, I'm sure you have other things to do today."

"Believe me it's no problem, I didn't have much planned for today anyway. Why don't you come over, you can use the shower and I will whip us up some lunch." Cliff knew this wasn't a thought out plan on his part. How was he going to concentrate while she was naked in his shower? Could he trust himself? He promised his friend that he would watch out for her, and that he wasn't interested in getting involved. Dumb mistake buddy. He cursed himself.

Serena thought about his offer and decided to accept. It wasn't like she was going over to sleep with him, just use his shower and eat lunch. "Well, if I won't be a bother, then I'll take you up on your offer. Let me throw together a bag and I will meet you downstairs in about ten minutes."

After Cliff left, Serena went over to the book and quietly whispered. "James what in the world was that hideous noise? Don't ever do that again, you scared the crap out of me."

"I was just trying to get your attention," confessed James. "I could sense some strong smoldering force in the room, and I didn't want to be in this location when things got really heated up."

Serena hysterically chuckled. "Whatever do you mean? Nothing was happening," She lied.

"Tsk , tsk, tsk ," mumbled James. "You seem to be forgetting that I can read your brain waves, feel the energy and sense the connections, and I will tell you the energy level was high, and you were almost connected."

"Whatever, James, you are delirious," Serena said with a shrug. "You can believe what you like. Now if you excuse me I have a date with a hot, wet shower. Oh, and next time, try calling my name and be less dramatic," Serena expressed, tossing items into a tote.

James laughed. "I could but my way is so much more fun. Really Serena a spider?"

"You're not very funny," Serena quietly yelled, trying to

keep her voice low. "By the way I have some information I got from Cliff and might share it with you later tonight, that is if you behave yourself." Serena said with a smirk on her face. "Bye," Serena said as she closed the door.

Cliff was patiently waiting for Serena at the bottom of the stairs. He swore he had heard her talking but she could have been on the phone, so he shrugged it off. Cliff offered to drive her, but she opted to follow him in case she wanted to leave.

Serena was ready to go when all of a sudden, Cliff appeared next to her car and handed her a gift. "What is this for?" She asked, her smile full of curiosity.

"Open it up and see. It wouldn't be a surprise if I told you what it was, would it?" Cliff answered.

He leaned into the driver's side window while Serena opened up her gift. His closeness made Serena a little uncomfortable, so she tried concentrating on opening her package. She was surprised to see a new pair of headphones and tan pair of Oakley Sunglasses. He had come through on his promise. At that moment in time, Serena felt the bricks guarding her heart shift a little more, as she turned to face Cliff to thank him. "I don't know what to say; thank you so much for remembering. I was missing my Oakley's and the music out of my old ear buds sounds a little distorted."

"You're very welcome, I always keep my word, or, at least, I try to," Cliff commented.

She found herself so close she could feel his breath on her face. It would just take a small movement and her lips could be exploring his. But it was all short-lived when a car horn sounded, and Serena frowned as a little blond in a Chevy Convertible drove by and blew him a kiss. Cliff looked up and gave her a quick wave.

Serena didn't know why, but she felt the jealously bug crawling on her and it made her uncomfortable. She would have to have feelings and care about someone for that to affect her, and she wasn't sure she was ready for that yet. It had only been a little over a month since Kevin and she had split up. So she pretended to tuck the feelings away and shrugged it off. It was none of her business anyway. It wasn't like they were an item, so he had the right to wave at any little bimbo he chose. This made Serena feel dumpy as she sat there feeling like a beach bum. A little agitated, she asked. "Do you think we could get going? I am really in need of a shower."

"Understand, even though you look pretty enough to me?" Cliff said in a flirtatious manner.

Serena, slightly red and embarrassed spoke after a nervous laugh. "Thanks for the compliment, but either you are being very kind or you need glasses."

"Just telling it as I see it," Cliff remarked, walking back to his truck.

As he led her down Franklin Street onto Marine Drive, Serena took in her surroundings the best she could, while driving. People were out walking the streets; tourists checking out the gift shops looking for the perfect souvenir to add to their collection or looking for the four-star restaurant, recommended by their hotel concierge. Others were going into one of the many museums to be fulfilled with an abundance of historical data.

What a beautiful little city. She definitely needed to spend a day as a tourist and take in what it had to offer. Focusing herself on the scenery around her instead on her destination, helped to calm her nerves. Why was she so nervous? She wasn't going to have sex with the man, just use his shower and eat a little lunch. It was no big deal, Serena told herself. There had been some close calls today so she was going to have to stay on guard. That would be easy right? Trying to not dwell on it, Serena tried to take mental notes of the streets they were turning onto so she could find her way back. He took a Right on 37th off of Marine, up a steep hill for a bit and a quick right onto Duane. Serena was captivated by the beautiful little neighborhood and exceptional view. What a perfect place to live, she thought.

She pulled into the driveway next to Cliff, and beside it sat the cutest light green and tan two-story cottage shaped house. The yard was well kept, nice but simple; a little lawn and four flower pots overflowed with a variety of exquisite plants threaded color throughout the yard. She especially liked the stepping stones that led up to the porch; each one had a different ship etched in it. The porch held a little bistro table and chairs and another planter containing a large fern.

Standing on the porch and looking out into the yard, Serena felt so connected here and wanted to embrace the moment. "What an awesome place." Serena said smiling while turning to Cliff. "I love the neighborhood it's so quaint. I bet you know all your neighbors, have weekend BBQs and summer street dances."

"It's pretty nice, I am glad you like it." Cliff answered. "I don't know all of them, but some of us get together now and then to barbecue. We watch out for one other, there is a neighborhood watch meeting once a month and we take turns hosting the meeting. There hasn't been much crime up here. We are fortunate to live just down the street from a famous monumental house, so this area is pretty well patrolled. Once in a while, they will catch a kid trying to break past the boundaries of the house, or a young adult paying off a bet or meeting some kind of initiation, by trying to finagle his way inside. Never anything serious, but it is a nuisance for the people that live there." Cliff opened the door and motioned for Serena to come in. "Let me show you where the shower is and then I'll get lunch started."

8) CLIFF'S HOME

Serena followed Cliff through a small foyer where pictures, probably of family and friends, welcomed you in. An antique rack took your hat and coat, and a small table held a ceramic vase and a matching plate, filled with a collection of keys, a wallet and eyeglasses. Through the foyer, Serena gazed in at the grand staircase directly in front of her. It was beautiful, both the steps and banister were crafted in dark hardwood and with the white wall contrast, the picture was complete. Everywhere Serena looked she found another area that gave the home life. She especially liked the large fluffy seat pillows in colors of tan and brown, situated in a built-in seat that was wrapped around large curved windows. She could imagine a big lazy cat stretched out, basking in the early morning sun. The plank walls and the high beam ceilings embodied the magnificent features of the house; very attractive with a masculine touch. Serena followed Cliff up the stairs to a large bathroom at the end of a small hallway.

"Here is your shower my dear," teased Cliff as he bowed to Serena. He hung a towel outside the shower and gave her brief instructions on how to use it.

"Thank you, I do so appreciate it," Serena said, only half

paying attention while the rest of her was checking out the room. There was an open enormous stone shower, probably the size of her entire bathroom in her apartment. She especially loved the porcelain water basin sitting on top of a black walnut granite counter top. The room was modern but still held true to the homey flair.

Cliff pointed to the shelf in the corner of the shower. "I imagine you brought your own, but you are welcome to use the shampoo and shower gel. It's all natural and scent is soft and light. Leave the door cracked and yell if you need anything, I should be able to hear you. I'll be in the kitchen playing chef," Cliff announced as he exited the bathroom.

Serena stared at her reflection in the mirror. Smiling, she thought, he definitely needed glasses. She felt unguarded and vulnerable so dismissing his request, she closed and locked the door. She undressed and stepped into the stall and in less than two minutes, an indoor waterfall temporarily took her away from her jumbled thoughts and uneasy feelings.

Downstairs, Cliff was busy in the kitchen trying to keep his mind on cooking instead of a naked Serena upstairs in his shower. Letting his mind drift for a moment, he wondered what it be like to touch her soft skin, kiss those sexy lips and let his fingers get tangled in her hair. Brody's bark brought Cliff back into the present, good thing too, because he had almost burnt his grilled cheese sandwiches. "Okay boy, I haven't forgotten about you, just be patient and we'll get to the beach soon."

Almost done with her shower, Serena noticed the shower massage and thought how good it would feel on her sore and aching muscles. As she stretched to adjust the shower head, she started to slip and grabbed on to the hose to keep herself from falling. That move, however, caused her body to twist around. The good news was she had prevented herself from falling but the bad news was that somehow she had managed to get her hair tangled in the heat control knob. Serena couldn't reach around and turn off the water or untangle her hair so she did the only thing she could and called for help. "Cliff, could you please come here?" After five minutes and no answer, Serena called again but this time a little louder and a little more urgency in her voice. At this point, she didn't care if she alarmed him; her body was starting to feel like a prune.

Downstairs, upon hearing Serena calling his name, Cliff turned off the burners and darted up the stairs with Brody dead on his heels. Arriving outside of the bathroom he turned the knob only to find it was locked. "What did you lock the door for? I thought I told to you to leave it cracked," Cliff said. He was a little irritated with her that she didn't trust him.

"I don't know; I just did," Serena whined.

"Is everything okay in there?" Cliff asked, curious as to why she had called him.

"It depends on what you call okay," Serena answered. "I'm not hurt but my hair is tangled around the temperature knob and I am standing with my back to the shower. I can't reach the handle to shut off the water and my skin is turning into leather," Serena reported, with a whine in her voice. "Please get me out of here."

"I have to go downstairs and get the keys; I'll be back in a few. Hang on," commanded Cliff.

"I have no other choice, it's not like I can go anywhere," Serena snapped, with a touch of sarcasm in her voice.

"You know Serena, sarcasm isn't pretty on you," Cliff yelled though the door, then turned to go get the keys.

Serena, not at all feeling in her happy place at that moment, threw eye daggers at the closed door.

Cliff went downstairs to find the keys while trying to picture an image in his mind derived from the description Serena had given to him. But all he could see was a beautiful, naked, redhead, dripping wet held captive in his bathroom. Every man's fantasy and he had promised Tom that he was trustworthy and wasn't interested. Dumb, dumb, dumb. It was getting harder and harder to reel in his hormones where Serena was concerned, and this mishap for sure was going to put them to the test.

It seemed like forever but within ten minutes Serena heard the key in the lock and watched as the door pushed open. "STOP!" Serena demanded. "Could you please cover your eyes?" she asked.

Cliff stopped abruptly. "I could but wouldn't that make it a little hard for me to see what I was doing?" Cliff stated. He wasn't about to reveal to her that he had already got a quick peek Even if he covered his eyes he wouldn't be able to hide the effect she had on him.

Serena thought for a minute. "How about if you turn to the wall and walk sideways to the shower, cover your eyes and I will guide you the rest of the way." Cliff, following Serena's absurd request, was able to get to her, turn the water off and hand her a towel.

Serena, now feeling less exposed wrapped in a towel, stood there trying to be patient while Cliff studied the situation.

"If you wanted me to join you in the shower all you had to do is ask, instead of going through such drastic measures," Cliff snickered.

Serena already embarrassed and totally not impressed by Cliff's humor, squinched her face up and offered him a fake smile. He was lucky she was a respectable lady because she could have thrown out some unrespectable verbiage, followed by an unkind hand gesture. Instead, she composed herself the best she could with the predicament she was in, took a deep breath and commented, "Very funny, could you please stop finding such humor in my unsettling predicament and get my hair untangled. I think your shower and I have bonded long enough."

"Sorry," Cliff said, sensing Serena's frustration. "I was just trying to lighten the mood, but I would probably feel the same if our places were switched."

"You sure did a good job here," Cliff commented, after analyzing the situation. "How in the world did you get it wrapped so tight?" Cliff asked, attempting to untangle the wet hair.

"I wanted to use the shower massage and I almost slipped reaching up for it, so I grabbed the hose and somehow twisted around and here I am, pretty crazy," answered Serena.

"So how bad is it?" Serena asked?

"Not too bad, nothing that a pair of scissors can't fix,." Cliff answered, hiding a grin.

"You're kidding right?" Serena asked, hoping he was just kidding. "Please tell me that you won't have to cut my hair"

"Don't worry; I think I can get most of it out," Cliff chuckled

Serena who was getting irritated and tired of standing in one place was not at all amused by Cliff humor. "Do you moonlight as a sadistic comedian? I myself cannot find any humor in this, I don't mean to sound like a bitch but I am cold and tired, and just want out of here!"

Cliff heard Serena talking, but what she had said didn't quite register. He was trying to focus on the task at hand, instead of her, who smelled of sweet honeysuckle and was inches away from him naked under a towel. It would be so easy to get tangled up in her, instead of untangling her hair. As alluring as that thought sounded, Cliff turned his mind back to the tangled mess. "There," Cliff said, "you're free, I was able to get most of the hair out."

Serena was so grateful to be free and just in time. Having Cliff so close was so intoxicating to her senses that she was nearing the edge of her sanity. Not trusting herself Serena stepped back to put distance between them, she had very little self-control left and was on the verge of throwing herself on him. So pathetic Serena thought, she definitely needed some serious counseling. "Thank you so much," Serena said sincerely. "Sorry to be such a pain. I can't believe that happened. I can handle it from here; I'll see you downstairs in a few."

Cliff who was oblivious to his surroundings was entranced by the beautiful mermaid in his shower. Her wild hair was wet and stuck to her luscious wet body, while glistening drops of water, slowly flowed down her leg. He wanted to drink that moisture from her skin. He could so imagine her soft subtle body pressed up against him.

Serena waved her hand in front of him and called to him hoping to pull him out of his trance. She wanted him to stop staring at her, like a man ready to devour a prime rib.

Hearing Serena's voice brought Cliff back to the surface. Busted! He cleared his throat and said, "Um, I'll just go finish lunch," he said, hurrying out the door. "Please do me a favor and don't lock the door this time," Cliff commented, as he closed the door behind him.

After Cliff left, Serena dressed, dried her hair and lightly applied a little makeup, then headed downstairs to find him. She just followed the aroma to the kitchen. By this time she was quite hungry, and remembered she hadn't eaten anything except some cereal for breakfast. Her stomach was telling her it had been way too long.

She found Cliff by the stove flipping over something that looked a lot liked grilled cheese. Feeling her presence he turned around and what he saw almost took his breath away. He nearly dropped the sandwich on the floor, especially after an image of her naked body flashed in his mind.

Serena, noticing Cliffs almost mishap, turned her head so he couldn't see her grin. She was also a little taken in by him standing in the kitchen barefoot, tight jeans and no shirt. Still a little unsettled, Serena pulled in her emotions and entered into the room.

"Yum, something smells really good, can I help with anything?" Serena asked.

Cliff, still trying to regain control on his emotions, answered, "everything is done; go take a seat at the table. I just need to put the soup in bowls."

"Sounds good," Serena said, walking over to the table, also trying to maintain her emotions, which seemed to be flying in all directions.

"What can I get you to drink?" Cliff asked, setting the soup on the table. "I have soda, water, juice or if it's something a little harder you desire, I have wine or beer."

Serena's face turned two shades of red when an image of what she desired formed in her head. Where was her mind? Maybe it was lack of sex. She felt so embarrassed. Control Serena, control.

As Cliff noticed the look on Serena's face, the color almost matching her hair, he realized what he had just said. He could feel the sexual tension in the room and it was probably best not to bring attention to his previous comment. He would have to be more conscious of what he said in the future.

Serena, recovering from the uncomfortable moment, answered, "Just water is fine; if you point me in the direction of the glasses I can help myself."

"You just sit; you're my guest I'll get it," Cliff gently instructed, getting ice waters for both of them and joining her at the table. Serena took in her surroundings; the kitchen was a chef's dream, very spacious, and the design layout was intriguing. An assortment of pots and pans dangled around an island in the center of the room. There was a double oven, side by side fridge, a large sink, all in stainless steel and more than enough cupboard space. It was so beautiful.

"Thank you for lunch, it looks delicious." Serena said. "It's been awhile since I've had a grilled cheese sandwich and tomato soup. Mom used to make it on stormy days and also when we had a bad day. It's great comfort food."

"You're welcome," Cliff said. "I figured you can't go wrong with that combo."

"What a beautiful house, did you remodel it yourself?" Serena asked, looking around the room.

"Thank you, I did a lot of it but I can't take all the credit,"

"You see, my late Uncle Michael left this house to my brothers and me, but at the time none of us were interested or ready to settle into a house, so it sat for many years. Those empty years took a toll on her. By the time I was ready to settle down, the house was falling apart and needed a lot of work and tender care. I bought out my brother's share and took ownership. We put a lot of sweat and hard work into her. I wanted to give her a modern flair and still preserve the historical features."

"I think you did just that. It's perfect Cliff," commented Serena. "Can I ask what made you want to settle down?" Serena asked, her curiosity lurking.

Cliff , whose eyes were fixed on Serena and contemplating on how much he wanted to share, put on a sober face and answered her. "I thought my ex-girlfriend Tandy, was the one I wanted to spend my life with." Cliff sighed and continued. "But after three years of living with someone who was so controlling had trust issues and was very materialistic, I realize she wasn't the one. The last year we were together it was like a volleyball game of fight and make-up. Nothing I did was ever good enough for her. I could never seem to please her, no matter how hard I tried. So I asked her to leave, and she confessed she was glad I did because she wanted to end the relationship. We parted on good terms. It's been a little over a year and I've never looked back."

Cliff picked up the dishes and carried them to the sink. "So here Brody and I live as bachelors in this big house," Cliff said, expressing the comment with open arms.

Serena, listening to Cliff share, thought to herself what a fool Tandy was. She lost it all, an amazing man and a fantastic house. But Serena knew all too well that things were not always as they seemed. That thought brought Kevin up to the forefront of her mind.

Cliff's voice brought Serena back to the present and she pushed Kevin into a vacant closet in her brain. "Can I get you anything else?"

"No thank you, that was perfect, more than enough." Serena answered patting her stomach. "You make a mean grilled cheese sandwich."

Smiling, Cliff said, "that's nothing you should taste my steak off the barbee, I hear it's the talk of the neighborhood."

"Well," Serena said, taking her glass and joining Cliff at the sink. "Nothing like a good steak. I would love to come the next time you have a barbecue."

"Consider yourself invited," Cliff said already planning so he could see Serena again. "It's probably about time the neighbors got a taste of down home cooking," Cliff boasted with a laugh. Tom did ask him to check in on her, he didn't say where she had to be, Cliff thought to himself.

"I would like that. I am off on Sundays but Saturday afternoons will work also," Serena said, trying not to sound overly excited. She really enjoyed being around Cliff. Even though he did make her nervous, she still felt comfortable and safe around him. Maybe they could just be friends, she thought.

"Let me clean up," Serena said nudging him away from the sink. "You made the meal and let me use your awesome shower, it's the least I can do. I won't take no for an answer," Serena said, pushing Cliff further away. "Go take Brody outside or something."

"Okay Brody," laughed Cliff. "You heard the lady, let's go boy." Brody didn't need any coaching, he grabbed his ball and with his tail wagging, dog and man went out to play.

"Whew!" Serena said, feeling the temperature in the room drop considerably as the door closed behind them. Things were definitely starting to brew between them. Serena needed time to regroup and get her feelings under control. She really needed to get home and go through the shop. She wanted to be prepared and, at least, appear somewhat knowledgeable tomorrow. There was a lot to learn. Serena also wanted to talk to James and do more research if she had time. Too bad he didn't have a cell phone on him; she'd call and say hi. She laughed at the strange thought.

She did want to walk out those glass doors leading to the backyard and embrace the breathtaking view. That's exactly what she was planning to do right after the dishes were done.

Cliff was relieved to break away from the heated tension. Tossing the ball was good for both man and dog, Brody was getting exercise and it gave Cliff time to gather his thoughts and put them into perspective. What was it about that redhead that got his senses flying and his emotions in a whirlwind? Was it because he was drawn to her, or was it because he hadn't really dated or connected much with any women in the past year? He did agree that he felt something for her and enjoyed having Serena at his house. For some crazy reason, he was already trying to get her to come back. He really should stay focused. This connection couldn't go further than friendship. Not now anyway.

Stepping out on the deck Serena welcomed the light brisk air and soft coastal wind. Standing in place, she could feel the rays of the sun softly kiss her face. Just as she had expected, the view of the river was absolutely spectacular. Looking off the deck she watched the connection between Cliff and Brody. Serena could see the bonding love and enduring friendship they had built. It was definitely a Kodak moment and her sentimental side released a lonely tear. She quickly wiped it away and gave a wave to the duo.

Cliff stopped short and almost tripped over Brody as he gazed up towards the deck at the beautiful goddess. Her fiery red hair was glistening in the sunlight and a few loose curls were dancing in the wind. "Hi," Cliff said as he returned the wave. "Could you please hold that pose while I get out my phone, I would like to take your picture? You look so beautiful standing there in the sunlight."

Serena didn't know how to respond to that, she tried to hide the shock she was experiencing. It had been awhile since a man had told her that and really meant it. Serena; speechless, just nodded her head and smiled.

"Perfect," Cliff stated, as he took a couple pictures from different angles. "Thanks, I'll text them to you. Let me toss the ball for Brody one last time and we will be up to join you." Cliff, laughing, picked up the ball Brody had dropped at his feet. "I swear if it were up to him we would be here for hours and my arm would wear out long before he would." he said, while giving the ball one last toss.

Serena felt her stomach fill up with butterflies and her body tingled with goose bumps as Cliff came up to stand beside her. She needed to pull herself together but herself seemed to fly south every time he came near her. "What a beautiful view," Serena said, gazing out at the river and breaking the silence lingering between them. "I could stay here for hours," Serena added, not wanting to look away; afraid of what would happen if she looked directly at him.

"It is, in fact, one of the major reasons I decided to keep this house," Cliff said, also taking in the view. "I do a lot of my thinking here, especially when there is a troubling issue brewing. "

"Do you ever solve any of them?" Serena asked

"Most of them, some take longer than others and some I let go."

"Enough about me, seems like I've been doing most of the talking. Tell me about Serena;" Cliff said.

That comment totally caught Serena off guard. She wasn't sure how she felt talking about her life with him. It was unsettling to her, going to that level so soon. She felt safer staying on the surface, going too deep was not a place she wanted to go. So instead of looking at him, Serena pretended to be locked in the view, facing him would only make her more vulnerable while she talked

"There's not a lot to tell," started Serena. "I am pretty simple, don't really lead a complicated life," '*strange yes, but not complicated*,' Serena thought to herself. "I have amazing friends and a loving family which I treasure very much. Of course, there's Tom who has been like a brother to me. Tess, my sister who is my best friend, we are like this." Serena said crossing her fingers on her right hand, showing the unity in their relationship. I have two precious nieces that I totally adore and enjoy spoiling. "Hmm, let's see," Serena continued, starting to relax a little, but still keeping it light. "I am acting CEO of my father's coffee company. He had a minor stroke a couple years ago and I stepped in to help him out, never dreaming that it would become permanent." Serena was thankful for the sunglasses that were hiding the sudden sadness in her eyes. She gave herself a moment to composed the hidden emotion before going on.

"Dad says someday he'll be back, I hope that's true. He was planning on it this year but the doctor added another year to his recovery. I can remember that day when I first heard the news; it was the worst day of my life." Serena said, pausing to take a breath. "The damage was minimal because he was taken to the hospital immediately. But we didn't find that out until the next day. Never had twenty-four hours passed so slow and painfully."

Serena felt Cliff's touch on her arm and at first she wanted to pull away but instead, she welcomed the security it brought to her, and took comfort in his touch. "Anyway," Serena continued, "I run the company but Dad is there if I need him."

"Three and a half years ago I met the man of my dreams, or so I thought at the time. But it sadly turned out that I was wrong, he was a cheat and a liar. One morning out of the blue he decided he didn't want to be in the relationship any longer. That was probably the second worst day of my life. Good thing I could count on my sister to bring me wine and sit with me through the pain and tears." Serena took a deep sigh as she briefly relived that day in her mind before going on.

"A couple years ago my dear Aunt Caroline (God rest her soul), passed away at a young age of fifty-three from cancer. She had willed her store, "Books on the Corner" to her daughter Lucy but it was too much for her. I was listed second in the will, so here I am, starting a new life and new job in Astoria. I'm still having a hard time adjusting to the move and not having my family near, especially my sister," Serena admitted.

Cliff had heard the pain in Serena's voice and wanted to take it all away. He took her arm, turned her towards him and wrapped his arms around her. He removed her sunglasses and when their eyes met, the moment took them away.

Serena, a little shaken by the movement, tried to think logically. He's was just a friend giving her a hug but when he removed the glasses and wiped away a stray tear, all her logic was gone. Then when his lips found hers, Serena was also gone. It was obvious Miss Conscience was tanning in the Bahamas because the Devil was steering this vehicle. The pent up electricity burned through them, letting loose sparks of excitement. Both of them knowing it was wrong, but not caring or wanting to stop. Their bodies could not get close enough and their souls couldn't seem to get deep enough as they kissed and explored, tasting what each other was offering. Their bodies were unaware that their subconscious minds were venturing towards a sizzling desire of wanting more.

Serena was reeling from the intoxication of his kisses. It felt so right, even her body was in agreement. Sensing she was moving too fast, Serena pulled herself away. Damn, Miss Conscience cut her vacation short. Touching her wet swollen lips she tried to shake off the sensual induced coma. "What am I doing?" she said, stepping back to put some distance between them as she regrouped.

Cliff, slowing coming back to reality and adjusting to the awkward moment, replied, "I think it's called kissing," he said with a sexy grin.

Serena, who was still trying to adjust, commented, "I know what we were doing, but this should never have happened. I barely know you and I am not ready to get into another relationship this soon . I really need to get going," Serena said, hurrying towards the door.

"Serena," Cliff called out. "Please wait." He walked over to her and took both her hands in his. Facing her he said, "I am sorry this made you uncomfortable, I am not going to say I'm sorry it happened. We both know there is something here pulling us together that we can't deny. Let's just take it slow and explore the possibilities." Looking into her frightened eyes, he could see the pain she was still enduring from her past relationship, and the last thing Cliff wanted to do was scare her away. "I would like to see you again, I promise hands off, Cliff said with a smile, putting his out in front of him.

Serena needed some time. Her emotions were doing acrobatics and she wasn't sure which one had the most control, so she didn't want to commit to anything. Looking up at Cliff, trying to hide the confused look on her face, she forced a smile and stated, "I can't agree to that now, I need more time to figure out how I am feeling. Thank you for a lovely time," Serena said as she went off to gather her belongings.

Cliff met Serena at the door. "I am going to take Brody to the beach. If you like, you can follow me back," he offered.

Serena wanted to protest, she was pretty sure she could find her way back but in her state of mind it was best to follow him. "Thank you," Serena answered. She gave Brody a hug, said her goodbyes and escaped to her SUV. Feeling safe and less exposed, Serena collected herself and by the time they were back at the shop, she felt almost normal again. That was until she noticed the door to the shop was wide open. Panic poured through her as she ran to the shop. Cliff started running after her with Brody barking and close behind him.

Cliff found her inside sitting on the floor with a book in her hand. He watched as she put it up to her face and called out. "James, are you ok? Please tell me you're ok," Serena said, clutching the book.

9) THE BREAK-IN

Cliff watched in bewilderment at Serena, who was obviously very upset, sitting on the ground talking to a book. He ran his fingers through his hair, as he tried to figure out why she was so concerned about a book. But right now there were more serious matters to contend with, like the break in. Given the unstable condition that Serena was in, he was going to have to take control of the situation.

"Serena, honey," Cliff said in a calm soft voice as he went to help her off the floor. "Why don't you give me the book before your hands lose their circulation from the death grip you have on it."

Serena, trying to pull herself together and reluctant to let go of the book, looked up at Cliff and replied, "I would like to hold on to it for a while. It has sentimental value and I would have been devastated if something had happened to it."

Cliff got a funny look on his face as he read the title of the book out loud. "Trust, Honor and Obey?" Looking at Serena, he asked, "Are you sure you have the right book?"

Serena realized by the confused look on Cliff's face, he was trying hard to comprehend why she was so obsessed with an ordinary book. Trying to seem inconspicuous, she whispered to James out of the side of her month. "I could use some help here." Serena, repeating James's words, answered Cliff. "It's not the book itself, it's just this book has made it through many generations in my family." Which was mostly true, Serena thought. She just hated to lie but she wasn't about to tell him the truth.

Cliff briefly examined the book. To him, it seemed in fairly good condition for supposedly being around for many years. But instead of questioning Serena about it now, he decided to concentrate on more important matters at hand. He was going to discuss this more in detail with her later. He was sure, there was something she wasn't telling him. Cliff turned to Serena and was relieved to see she had loosened her grip on the book a little. "We probably should report this to the police and..." but before he could finish his sentence Serena interrupted.

"I don't think that's necessary, it doesn't look like anything else was disturbed," Serena said, taking a cursory look around her shop. "Why don't we walk around and check things out, then watch the store video. I promise if we see anything disturbing I will call the police."

Cliff agreed but under protest. Since it wasn't his store he'd wait to see if or what they found before raising the issue. Sternly, he stated, "I will agree, under the condition that you let me change your locks tonight and if we see something that could put you in danger, I **am**, calling the police!" Cliff stressed to Serena.

Serena nodded in agreement. "I will take a look upstairs and you can have the downstairs," Serena said as she turned and started for the stairs, the book, safe in her right hand. But when she got to the bottom of the stairs she turned to look back at him and found herself wrapped in his arms as they softly collided. Oh no here they were again, Serena thought, their bodies molded together. For a temporary second, all Serena could think about was how her body fit perfectly against his warm hard body. She felt so secure and protected wrapped in his strong arms. Then she suddenly remembered what she was doing and pulled herself away. Agitated with herself, she placed her left hand on her left hip and questioned Cliff. "I thought I was taking the upstairs and you were going to search the downstairs."

"That's what you said, but I didn't say I agreed to it," he smirked. "I think we should stay together in case there is someone else hiding in here."

Serena wasn't sure if she was touched by his protectiveness or annoyed. She knew there wasn't cause for alarm. James had told her that he had heard only two voices and that as far as he could tell by their muffled whispering, they were only after the book. However, she couldn't very well tell that to Cliff, so she let him escort her up the stairs.

She had left her apartment door unlocked but was sure it had been shut when she left. It was now wide open. Cliff stepped in front of her and told her to wait in the hall while he checked it out.

So Serena stood outside the door and nervously waited.

"Come on in," Cliff said, "It doesn't look like anything was disturbed, but just to be safe you probably shouldn't touch anything in case they left their fingerprints," he stressed.

Chills ran through Serena as she stepped into her apartment. She stood there in shock with her arms folded in front of her, looking at her new place. There didn't appear to be any signs that someone had been there, but just knowing strangers had invited themselves into her personal space, left her with an uneasy feeling.

Cliff must have sensed her emotional turmoil because he came up behind her and put his arm around her. He laid her head against his shoulder and asked with tenderness in his voice, "Are you going to be alright? If you want, Brody and I can stay with you tonight."

Serena, feeling comfort in his embrace, wanted nothing more than to have him stay with her but somewhere inside she heard a little voice telling her it was a bad idea. Especially when his warm breath so close to her ear, was sending her hormones dancing. Turning to face Cliff, Serena answered. "Thank you for your offer but I think I will be fine." Taking a deep breath Serena continued. "'It's not only that they tried to steal the book but they also trespassed into my apartment, I feel personally violated. Let's go downstairs and look around then watch the video, I am curious to see what the intruders did in here."

After walking around downstairs and relieved nothing looked out of place or disturbed, they ventured into the coffee shop. "Want one?" Serena asked as she set her shaken mind on making coffee. A simple no-brainer task, one she was confident in handling.

"Sure, hit me with a double shot of espresso, I could use an energy burst," Cliff answered.

They took their coffees to the main lobby. Cliff took a seat on the sofa while Serena retrieved the tape out of the camera, put in the VCR and attempted to get it to work. It must have belonged to her aunt because Serena was pretty sure they were extinct.

Brody sat down by his master and plopped his head in his lap. Cliff scratched behind his ears and told him there would still be time to play at the beach. Just hold on just a little longer. They would have to leave soon if they wanted to make it to the beach before sunset. Cliff really didn't feel comfortable leaving Serena here at night. He was going to work on her to let him stay. He then turned his attention back to the sweet red head.

Serena was still preoccupied with trying to get the VCR controls to cooperate with her. She was used to new technology and the VCR was far from it. Note to self... Update security. Finally, after fighting with the remote and recorder for fifteen minutes, she had succeeded in getting it to work.

Cliff and Serena watched as two people dressed in black with mask covered faces, approached the building. By the looks of their body shapes, they were able to tell that it was a man and woman tag team. The woman stood watch as the man successfully picked the lock. They spoke in a quiet whisper so it was difficult to hear what they were saying. As they walked into the shop, the woman headed off to check the downstairs, going straight for the self-help books. It was obvious they knew what they were looking for. The man called to her and pointed upstairs. What Serena didn't understand was why he thought the book was upstairs. She would have to check to see if her room was bugged. The team climbed the stairs to her apartment and Serena clenched her hands into fists, as she witnessed the strangers enter her apartment. Cliff, noticing Serena's reaction, took her hands in his and held them tight.

They continued watching the team as they searched through Serena's things. They went through cupboards and drawers and browsed the book shelves. When they entered Serena's room, she couldn't contain herself. "How dare they go in there and rummage through my personal items. I feel so violated. Do you know how much cleaning and disinfecting I am going to have to do? It gives me the creeps just thinking they touched my personal belongings," Serena cringed.

Cliff didn't know how to respond so he lightly squeezed her hands and continued to watch the video. The couple, upon entering the bedroom, noticed the book sitting on the nightstand. After sharing a whisper, the women walked over to the book. She quickly picked it up and then they both hurried out of the apartment.

The next part, Cliff had to rewind and watch several times. He couldn't believe what he was seeing. His eyes must be tired, he thought. He watched intensely as the man walked out the door of the shop and onto the sidewalk. The woman, who had the book in her hand was not so lucky. Each time she tried to go through the door, the book jumped out of her hand and onto the floor. This process repeated five times and then the man tried it with the same results. After realizing that they couldn't get the book out the door, the disgruntled team gave up and left the shop.

Oh my goodness, Serena thought to herself as she put her hand up to her mouth. How was she going to explain this to Cliff? She didn't know what to say to him. It was obvious that he was confused.

"That was pretty strange," was all she could come up with.

Cliff ran his fingers through his hair as he seemed to do when he was in deep thought, looked at Serena and reached out his hand and asked, "Could you please let me see the book for a moment?"

Reluctantly she handed it to him. She was surprised when he went to the door and reenacted the scene on the video. He tried three times to walk out the door, but the book jumped out of his hands, just like it had with the woman. With a perplexed look on his face, Cliff walked over to Serena. "You want to tell me something about this book?" Cliff asked, patiently waiting for an explanation.

Serena gave Cliff a wide smile as she tried to decide on what to say. "What do you want me to tell you about it? I have never seen it do that before," she answered.

Cliff knew she wasn't telling him the whole truth and was

getting a little discouraged with the entire thing. "Serena what is so important about this book? It is obvious that was the only thing they came for. Do you have any idea why they wanted it?"

Serena could tell Cliff was getting irritated with the situation and was looking for answers. Only she wasn't ready to give him a full explanation. Looking up at him as he gave her back the book, she made her best attempt to smooth things over for the time being. "You wouldn't believe me if I told you. Yes, there is something special about it but I don't know why anyone would want it. Look, Cliff, this has been a crazy day and Brody still needs to get to the beach. Can we please discuss this at another time? I'm tired and need to regroup before tomorrow. It's my first day on the job and I would like to seem somewhat coherent and alert.," Serena pleaded.

Cliff, realizing he wasn't going to get Serena to confess to anything tonight, answered with a slight hesitation. "Okay, I'll drop the subject, for now, that is if you will let us stay tonight. I can stop at the house and grab some clothes and food for Brody on my way back from the beach. I also want to change the locks on your front door. I'll even pick up a pizza on my way back."

Serena's better judgment was telling her it was not a good idea, but the thought of having him there tonight was comforting and she wouldn't have to tell him about the book, so she agreed. At least she would have a little time for herself and be able to check in with James while they were gone.

So after they left, Serena moved the sofa in front of the door and went from room to room inspecting the windows. She also made sure the back door was secure as well, and made a mental note to herself to call the security company tomorrow. After she felt somewhat safe, she sat down with a strong cup of coffee while trying to clear her head.

"Whew, I thought he would never leave." James exclaimed with a sigh. "You are going to have to tell him about me some time."

Serena not really wanting to deal with the thought of that task, replied, "I know, as soon as I think of the best way to tell him. It doesn't really matter anyway, because whatever I say he's going to think I'm crazy, which I am not sure that's too far from the truth," Serena stated.

"You are no crazier than I am Serena," commented James.

Serena knew James meant well but that wasn't much of a comfort to her coming from a talking book. "James, do you know why they wanted the book?" Serena asked, taking the book with her as she picked up the cups and headed into the coffee shop.

"I have no clue, I wish I could've heard what they were talking about but their voices were so quiet. Maybe they said something that might add a piece to the puzzle."

"I am going to take the video to a friend of mine in Portland, who is a technology wizard, and see if he can figure out a way to make the voices louder." Serena expressed to James. "If only we could tell who those people were, we might find the answers we are looking for. Was it luck they found the book or did they know where to go? I am going to check the room for bugs."

"Serena I am sorry that I've gotten you into this mess." James apologized. "I never meant for any of this to happen to you. I was hoping you could find out who I was and find a way to release me from this book. I just want to be free."

Serena felt sorry for the spirit and really wanted to help him; looking down at the book she commented. "It's all good, so my life is a little weird at times, at least, I can't say it is boring," Serena giggled. "I promise you I am going to spend more time researching and try hard to find out who did this to you. If we can answer that question we might get closer to finding how to release the spell. You know, maybe if I do tell Cliff, he'll help us too." Yeah, help her by calling the little men in their pretty white coats and wave as they take her away.

"By the way James," Serena continued. "I spoke with Cliff this morning and he shared some information that may help. I know this will sound crazy, but I believe he is your nephew. You both have the last name of Hallow. At one time he had five uncles, two died and two were disowned by the family, and one is happily married and comfortably retired. I am thinking that you might be one of the disowned ones. I know that sounds a little harsh and he didn't know any of the details, but he is going to ask his dad." Serena stated, pausing a moment to give James a chance to comment, but he was quiet. He was probably trying to process the information. "I could be totally wrong, but if we go on that assumption, at least, we have somewhere to start."

Serena was right; James was trying to wrap his mind around the thought. He wished he could remember, it frustrated him and there was nothing he could do about it. Could it be possible what Serena said is true? If so, why was he removed from his family? Even though he wanted his memory back, he was also afraid of what he might find out about himself. But for now, he would move on and hide his emotions from Serena. She had enough on her plate.

Trying to sound upbeat James commented. "Well, that good old boy might be my nephew, Serena you have to introduce us, please," James pleaded.

"I will in time, it's not going to be easy," Serena said, shaking her head at the absurd thought. "It's not like I will be introducing Cliff to one of my friends. If you haven't noticed yet James, you're a book. I haven't had much practice, correction; no practice in this so I need to think about how and when to tell him. You have to give me a little more time James. Now let's drop the subject, I need to get things done before Cliff gets back."

Down on the beach, as he walked with Brody, Cliff was glad to have a few minutes alone to think and process the last few hours. First, he had been thrown off balance after his sensual encounter with Serena at his house, and the little taste of her, only left him yearning for more. Luckily she was able to stop it before it went too far. She was right, they were moving too fast, he would have to be strong and keep this relationship strictly platonic. If only it was that easy.

Next, the incident at the bookstore, which Cliff's intuition told him Serena knew a lot more about the book than she was sharing. He wondered what secrets lie behind that mysterious lady? If only he could gain her trust so she would feel safe enough to confide in him. But he wasn't sure how to do that. There were so many questions he didn't have the answers to and probably wouldn't tonight. So as the clouds covered the semi blue sky and a light fog attempted to move in, Cliff and Brody left their peaceful surroundings.

Back at the shop Serena made her way through each section of the book area making mental notes and taking written notes on how the books were categorized. It shouldn't be too hard, once she learned the layout. She thought. Labels were located at the end of each row that identified the books in the alphabetical breakdown by Authors last name. Prices were clearly marked on each book. There was also a section that contained used books as well. The books in the children's corner were structured in the same way. Besides the books, all that was left were the souvenirs and specialty gifts, and they had little price tags attached.

Last of all, Serena went to the front desk to familiarize herself with the cash register but found that to be a challenge. Like the VCR, it should go to the antique haven for outdated equipment and be replaced by modern technology. But until then it would serve its purpose. She would have to ask Lucy to teach her how to operate the strange contraption if she planned on doing any sales transactions. The same wonderful gadget also occupied space at the sales counter in the coffee shop. Wonderful, she thought, that's where she'd be spending the majority of her time, except on Lucy's days off. Definitely updating that system would be high on her list. A loud knock startled Serena out of her business mode, and changing mental hats she went to greet her sleepover guests.

The two of them exchanged small talk while they ate their pizza, never mentioning the book or the video, which was clearly elephants in the room. After dinner, Cliff changed the locks on the main door while Serena went upstairs to the small guest bedroom to move her unpacked boxes so Cliff would have room to move around. The room itself wasn't much bigger than a large storage unit so even after the boxes were gone, the quarters would be a little cramped. Luckily she had kept her single bed, but gauging by the size and mentally measuring Cliff, the bed was going to be a bit small. Oh well, it would have to do. Trying to clear the thought of Cliff lying in any position, Serena made the bed and left to deal with the rest of her apartment.

Serena still had an unsettling feeling knowing strangers had been in her home. She went from room to room with her trusty disinfectant spray and cleaning cloths, hoping to rid her apartment of their presence. They had worn gloves so Serena didn't have to worry about covering up fingerprints. She spent extra time in her bedroom, it didn't matter to her that the video showed them in there for a short time, it was a sacred place to her. It gave her peace and comfort as she stripped the bed and vigorously scrubbed the furniture. She even took the clothes out of dresser drawers and put them in the laundry. After an hour, Serena was satisfied with her progress and felt more relaxed in her surroundings. She changed into some jogging pajamas and decided to see what Cliff was up to, as well as bring James upstairs. As she opened the door she noticed he was back at the door, trying to figure out why he couldn't get the book outside. Serena, looking out a small crack in the door watched as Cliff stuck his hand outside and back in, then ran his hand around the entire door jam. He even went as far as testing to see if it would happen with other books. Serena smiled as she thought about showing Cliff the video of himself when this was over. Maybe he wouldn't see the humor in it as she did. After he tired of the examination of the door, he gave up and locked it. That is when Serena came out of hiding.

"Hey," Cliff said, turning as he felt Serena enter the room

"Hey yourself," Serena said, walking over to the door to check on the new locks that Cliff had installed.

Cliff explained in detail and demonstrated how each lock worked. "I replaced your door knob; it has a double lock feature that takes two keys to unlock," Cliff said, handing Serena two keys. "I also added a cross-over lock bolt, which you can lock and unlock from both sides. Here is the key for the outside. There is now a chain on the door, more for your added security. Tomorrow I will change the locks on the back door. So what do you think?"

Serena was quite impressed with Cliff's handiwork. She was also touched by his thoughtfulness and caring demeanor.

Thinking to herself, she could get used to this, but wasn't going there now. "It's perfect Cliff, thank you so much, I feel safer already."

Happy that she was pleased, Cliff smiled and said. "That should keep any unwanted visitors out, and if there is an unknown secret passage, Brody will alert us. It should be an uneventful night."

Looking at Cliff she mentally painted an eventful night with him in her mind. She just wanted to climb into his arms and drown in the kisses that she could still taste on her lips. It would be so easy to melt in his embrace. She could get lost in his eyes and watch them take her into a forbidden fantasy, away from all her troubles and worries. Somewhere, only the two of them existed. Serena snapped out of her dream world when she heard Cliff call her name,

"Yes," she answered, unaware that this was the second time he had called her name.

"I was telling you about the door and I seemed to have lost you."

Serena looked at Cliff and answered with a yawn. "I am sorry Cliff. I am thoroughly exhausted and ready to call it a night."

Cliff could plainly see by the weariness in Serena's eyes and the weakness in her voice that she needed rest. He was hoping to get her to talk more about the book but that wasn't going to happen tonight. It had been a long day, and he was dragging a little himself.

"Why don't you head upstairs, I am going to take Brody out in the courtyard, do one more inspection throughout the shop and lock up. Good night," Cliff said as he playfully blew her a kiss.

Serena playing along caught the imaginary kiss and put it to her cheek. "Good night to you, sweet dreams and Cliff, I have been thinking about what you asked me, and I have decided that I would love to go on a date with you. However, I would like to wait a couple weeks." With that being said, Serena threw Cliff a big kiss and headed up the stairs.

Cliff was not expecting that and it threw him off guard as he caught her kiss but instead of his cheek, he placed it on his lips. He got Brody's leash and took him out for the last time that night. Cliff took a seat on a little bench as he gave Brody the freedom to mark his territory. "Oh Brody boy I've got it bad, Cliff said to his dog who stopped what he was doing and raised his head. It was like he understood every word. "I think I am starting to fall for her and we haven't even gone on an official date." Done with his duty, Brody came and sat down by his master and put his head in his lap. "What am I going to do? I told Tom I wasn't interested. Who was I fooling? That sexy redhead had my heart the first time I saw her. I probably should call Tom and confess just in case. Come on boy, let's go hit the sack." Even though Cliff was feeling tired, he was afraid it was going to be a long and restless night. Knowing Serena was in her bed just a few feet away, sleeping was going to be the furthest thing on his mind.

Serena was lying awake in her bed when she heard them come in. She was hoping to fall asleep before her overactive thoughts took hold. All she could think about was Cliff sleeping in the room next to hers.

Cliff, trying to be quiet, prepared himself for bed. Brody was happy just curling up on a spare rug. After an hour of tossing and turning, he realized that a restful night's sleep was not in the cards for him tonight. His mind kept wandering to the other room. Was she sleeping or thinking about him? Probably sleeping, considering how exhausted she was. He needed to derail his mind so he got out his phone and went through his email. There were a couple from his mom, one from his sister and a few concerning work matters. After giving attention to most of them, he looked at the clock to find it was 11:55. He needed to try to get some sleep, but first, he went to find a glass and water.

With a glass of water in hand and walking back to his room he was greeted by a strange presence. If he believed in ghosts, he would bet his money that one just floated by him. Maybe he was dreaming or better yet sleep walking, that had to be it. He watched as the floating object disappeared through the front door of Serena's apartment. He slapped his face a couple times in an attempt to wake up, he wasn't sure if it worked or not. He didn't feel any different. Well if he was asleep he was going to go back to bed and hope his dream pattern changed from ghosts to something more enjoyable, say a sassy red-headed hot number. Oh shit, he thought how will I survive tomorrow no cold shower? Great!

Sleep wasn't coming to Serena either. She was so exhausted. She should've been starring in a dream about now, instead of fantasying about the man in her house. Mr. Sandman made a late delivery around midnight, finally allowing her to quiet her brain and fall asleep. Serena found herself in the most bizarre dream, a strange combination involving her, Cliff and a spirit.

10) THE NEXT MORNING

Cliff who had managed to catch a few hours of sleep awoke suddenly staring right into the eyes of his beloved companion. "Brody boy, don't you think you could wait just a little longer?" He asked trying to focus. But Brody wasn't about to let that happen, he laid his head on the bed and looked at Cliff with his big puppy eyes. When he sensed Cliff was starting to fall asleep, he nudged his arm with his nose until he got his attention. "Okay, okay, boy you win but you'd better make it fast, it's still early and I could use a little more sleep."

As Cliff was sitting on the couch in the living room slipping his shoes, he thought he saw the same ghostly image again, only this time as it floated past, it waved at him. Shaking his head, he concluded that it was either his imagination or a play of colors from the sunrise, peeking through the bay window. He shrugged off the eerie feeling, grabbed Brody's leash and quietly left the apartment. Unaware that the ghostly figure he had just seen, might be a relative of his.

Cliff was surprised when he opened the back door and almost collided with Lucy.

A look of confusion played on Lucy's face when she looked

up to see Cliff standing in the doorway. She step to the side and entered the shop. She then turned and with a big smile on her face, said with a laugh. "Wow, when I called for your services all I got was a bill, when Serena calls she gets a sleep over."

Cliff was feeling quite uncomfortable dressed in his lounging joggings and light jacket zipped half way up and baring his chest. He could imagine what this must look like to Lucy.

Before Cliff could explain, Lucy put her hand out in front and commented with a big smile on her face. "No need for explanations. You two are consenting adults, and it's none of my business. What I would like to know is why my key doesn't work in the front door anymore?"

Cliff, relieved that Lucy had changed the subject, released a quiet sigh and answered her question. "There was a break in last night. I'll explain in more detail after I take Brody out," who was getting very impatient with his master.

Lucy a little shaken by the news, replied, "Sounds good. I'll go brew us some coffee, hurry back, don't keep me in suspense too long."

In less than ten minutes Lucy and Cliff were seated at a little table in the coffee shop. She quietly sat across from him nervously twisting her hands while Cliff briefly told her what had happened last night.

Lucy raised her hand up to her mouth, "Oh my goodness," she gasped. "Nothing like that has ever happened here. It just doesn't make sense. Why would they want a book?" She asked, as she sat pondering the question.

"I don't know," Cliff answered, not sure how to reply to the question. "Maybe Serena can give you more details. Right now I am going to take her some coffee, let her know you're here, then I need to go get the parts to fix the showers. Good seeing you Lucy, thanks for the coffee." Then he quickly exited the coffee shop to avoid any more questions.

Serena had awoken shortly after Cliff and Brody had left. She cleaned up the best she could without a shower, put on some casual clothes, lightly touched her face with a hint of makeup and gave her lips a little shine with a swipe of her cherry lip gloss. She was on her way down to get coffee when she met Cliff at the top of the stairs. He must have read her mind because the sweet man had brought her a cup. Her mind drifted as she took in the view. What a sexy sight with his tousled hair, unshaven face and no shirt under his jacket. It was enough to send Serena into a sensual coma. Why did he do this to her? When he was around her self-control took a sabbatical and her brain connections got all jumbled. Usually, she was a pretty level headed woman, and it scared her to think that someone could have this much effect on her. She didn't remember feeling this uneasy around Kevin.

Trying to shake off the moment, she graciously accepted the coffee. "Thank you so much for the coffee. You are my best friend today," Serena said with a laugh, trying to lighten the mood.

Cliff, captivated by the beauty of Serena and trying to keep his eyes off her glistening lips, replied, "You're welcome, Lucy made it. In fact, I almost collided with her at the back door this morning. I think she was a bit startled to see me and asked why her key didn't fit the front door. So I explained to her the best I could while we had coffee."

"Oh no I forgot to call Lucy!" Serena exclaimed unhappy with herself for forgetting such an important detail. "I was so caught up in the night's events that it totally slipped my mind," Serena said, walking back into her apartment.

Cliff, noting a look of concern on Serena's face, followed her in and intervened in her thoughts. "I'm sure she understands, given the circumstances. But be prepared, she'll probably be asking some questions," Cliff informed Serena.

Remembering the previous night's events, Serena wondered how much Cliff had told Lucy. As though he had read her mind, Cliff decided to have a little fun with Serena. "Don't worry I just stuck with the facts. I told her I spent the night and we had hot, crazy, wild sex until dawn," he said with a sly smile. Noticing Serena's wide eye expression, Cliff quickly confessed. "I was just kidding, I told her the truth, but don't worry, I didn't mention what was on the video. You can tell her if you like."

Serena was still reeling with the hot, sweaty sex comment and totally missed the last part. She turned her face away from Cliff as she tried to hide the excitement that ran through her.

Cliff watched Serena as she attempted to hide the effect he had on her. Stepping closer he gently lifted her chin and turned her face towards him. Looking into her smoldering eyes, he whispered in a soft sexy voice. "It's not to say I didn't think of taking you many times last night. I know we agreed to keep some distance between us, but the more I'm around you, the harder it is to resist you. Right now I want to run my fingers through your hair of fire, taste those delicious lips and devour every inch of your gorgeous body."

Serena could feel her body aching for Cliff's touch and before another word was said, she melted into his arms. They found themselves tangled together in a passionate embrace. They shared kisses so powerful that it felt like their bodies would ignite. But, as usual, the universe was always intervening. It kept shoving them together and pulling them apart. They were abruptly brought back to reality when they heard a voice calling from downstairs. It was Lucy calling for Serena.

Serena stepped back and put a finger up to his lips to shush Cliff and yelled down to Lucy. "Hey Luce, I'll be down in a couple minutes. Cliff is looking at my shower."

Cliff smiled at her as she threw out the lie to Lucy, her swollen lips and tangled hair showed the aftermath of their erotic encounter.

Serena hated to lie. She couldn't believe that they'd almost given in to temptation while Lucy was downstairs and James was close by. Where was her mind anyway? It was wrapped up in that sexy hot man standing inches from her.

She needed to get control of herself.

Disappointment shadowed Cliffs face. He didn't want to stop, but he could name all the reason why he should. Stepping closer to Serena, he took her in his arms, leaned her down and gave her a sensual kiss which sent her mind reeling again.

He set her upright and looked deep in her eyes and said, "This will be continued at a later time. You can bet on it." He gently teased her lips with his teeth and stepped away.

Serena was speechless. She definitely needed to get away from this man so she could find her mind again. Luckily she didn't have to respond, thankful for Cliff's change of subject about a dream he had.

Cliff didn't know why but he felt this uncontrollable urge to share his strange experience from last night. It would be a good tension breaker, which he thought, they both needed at this time. "I think I was sleepwalking or had a strange dream last night and again early this morning," he said, taking a sip of his now cold coffee and continued. "I got up for water close to midnight and a ghostly image floated by me, then I thought I saw the same image float by me again, just barely before sunrise. What's even stranger, I am pretty sure it waved at me."

Serena definitely wasn't prepared for this, choking on a sip of her coffee.

"Serena, are you alright?" Cliff said, rushing over to her side.

"It went down the wrong pipe." Serena tried to say in between coughing spells. "Wow, that was quite a dream," commented Serena after she recovered, trying to sound interested instead of shocked. "Maybe it was a combination of pizza and the weird events that happened last night." Serena said, hoping that Cliff would come to that same conclusion.

"You're probably right, but it seemed so real." Cliff said, running his fingers through his hair. "I should probably get going, I have lots to do, and it's a busy day for you as well. I'll be back later to fix the shower," he said with a smile.

A little sadness came over Serena as she watched Cliff gather up his things and call for Brody. She really had enjoyed having him here, but there was so much to do, and she needed some space from this man, until she decided how she felt. Right now it was probably lust, and that was the last thing she needed, right? She thought.

"Thanks for everything, and if I don't see you when you come back, I will call you later." Serena said, walking over to Cliff as she placed a soft kiss on his cheek and petted Brody. She let the moment dissolve into her as he closed the door behind him. Now she had to go down and face Lucy. She would need a strong cup of coffee for courage.

Downstairs Serena found Lucy in the romance section, adding new books to the collection. Looking up with a smile on her face she greeted Serena. "Morning cousin, sounds like you had quite the night and by the looks of you, the morning too."

"Morning to you to Luce, and if you are referring to Cliff, nothing happened. He just stayed with me because of the break-in, and slept in the spare bedroom." Serena said, trying to sound convincing.

"Hey sweetie, you don't have to answer to me, but if you ask me, Cliff's not a bad catch and I think you would be good for each other," Lucy admitted.

"He is a very nice man, but we are just friends, and I intend on keeping it that way." Serena stated. The words liar, liar went off in her head as her mind drifted back to the kisses they had shared earlier. "I was happy to have him here last night after what happened." Serena admitted, grabbing a book from the box and helping Lucy stock the shelves.

"Oh yes." Lucy said; a startled look showing on her face. "What happened last night? Cliff told me a little and said you might know more."

Serena stopped what she was doing to answer her cousin. "There isn't really much to tell. I went to Cliff's house to use his shower and he followed me back on his way to take Brody to the beach. When we arrived at the shop, we found the door open and checked out the shop. There didn't seem to be anything out of place. I would appreciate it though, if you would report anything out of the ordinary. I didn't feel the need to call the police and get tangled up in the red tape when nothing was stolen." Serena paused to gather her thoughts for the next part. "I am not sure what they were after or why the book was lying by the door. I am just grateful Cliff was with me and they were gone before we got here," finished Serena.

Reaching into her sweatshirt pocket she pulled out a set of keys and handed them to Lucy. "Here are the keys for the new locks on the front door. I'll be giving you new ones for the backdoor after Cliff has replaced the locks."

"Thanks," Lucy said, accepting the keys and placing them in her own pocket. "So are you ready to get started? We have a lot to cover before tomorrow."

Serena, giving Lucy her undivided attention answered. "I will be. Just let me grab a tablet and another cup of coffee and I'm all yours."

Heading to the coffee shop an eerie feeling overtook Serena as she noticed a man and a woman walk slowly pass the store window, paying strict attention to the inside of her shop.

Lucy turned around expecting to find Serena behind her. Instead, she noticed her walking towards the window, totally oblivious to what Lucy was saying.

"Hey, earth to Serena!" Lucy exclaimed, "Is everything alright?" She asked. "I seemed to have lost you for a couple of minutes."

Serena put on her happy face and turned to face Lucy. "Yes, everything is fine. I thought I saw a familiar face but I was wrong. Let's go get more coffee and you can show me the ropes," Serena said, linking her arm in Lucy's and heading to the coffee shop. "You can start by showing me how that WW2 cash register works." They both laughed and for the time being, Serena forgot all about the strange couple.

For the better part of the morning, they mostly stayed in the coffee shop. Serena had to admire Lucy; she had written out an agenda and touched on each task in detail from where everything was located down to the well-kept booking log. She was talking faster than Serena could take notes. Serena found that the cash register wasn't hard to operate, and Lucy did a happy dance when Serena announced that would be the first to get updated. Serena also shared with Lucy her other improvements she was hoping to make.

They were briefly interrupted by Cliff as he stuck his head in the coffee shop and greeted them. "Hi ladies, something told me I would find you in here. Well, Lucy, is she ready to go it solo?" he laughed.

Serena sent a sassy smile his way and a shiver ran through her as she walked past him to pet Brody.

"Hi Cliff," Lucy answered back. "She definitely is in the coffee shop. She already makes a mean espresso and can operate that old thing," she laughed, pointing to the cash register. "I think we have gone over most of the important things, and she's got enough notes to fall back on."

Serena, arms wrapped around Brody's neck, interjected. "Uh um, hey you two if you haven't noticed I happen to be in the room too and doing just fine. Thank you, Lucy, for the vote of confidence, I would probably be able to get by. Please promise me you aren't planning any surprise vacations anytime soon," Serena pleaded.

Lucy raised her right hand as if taking an oath and answered, "I promise I won't leave you on your own until your feel you are ready. As far as I know, we don't have any vacations scheduled until later this summer, so there is no need to worry."

Getting up off the floor and brushing the loose hairs off her clothes, she gave Cliff a playful look and teasingly said, "Don't you have a shower to fix or door lock to change?"

Cliff snickered. "Yeah I do." He answered with a smile. "Oh, by the way, I stopped by the deli and grabbed a couple extra sandwiches. I thought you ladies might be hungry, he said, handing Serena the bag.

"Thanks, that was very nice of you," Serena graciously answered. Taking the bag from Cliff she accidently brushed her hand lightly against his, sending electrifying currents up her arm. Unable to move Serena stood there frozen for the moment as she watched Cliff walked away until she was pulled back into reality by the sound of her name.

Serena, finding herself in an embarrassing moment again, turned to her cousin and answered. "I am sorry Luce, I must really need food, I think I almost blacked out there." Serena said, knowing it was just a half lie.

Lucy, who wasn't going to buy her excuse spoke up, "Uh huh, right…" Lucy said, nodding her head questioning Serena. "I saw the way you two looked at one another; friends don't look at one another like that," Lucy grinned, expressing herself. "Why can't you just admit that you like him? What harm is it anyway?"

Serena knew Lucy was right and she hated not being truthful to her, so she broke down and told her almost everything, leaving out a few of the intimate details. "I don't know why I am fighting it," Serena said taking a deep breath. "Maybe because it's too soon, either that or I am not ready and afraid of being hurt again," Serena admitted as a lonely tear drifted down her cheek.

Lucy walked over to her and embraced her in a hug. "Honey, it's going to be ok. Maybe you're mind isn't ready, but your heart is surely going in that direction." Lucy stepped back from Serena and brushed her hair out of her eyes, then said, "Serena, life isn't always easy and then when you put love into the equation it gets a little harder. I know you will do the right thing. Take it slow and see what happens. Now, I don't know about you but I am famished! Let's dig into those sandwiches."

Serena feeling much better now that she had someone to confide in, wiped her eyes and smiled at Lucy. "Thanks, Luce, for being here and caring. I really appreciate it. I love you cous," and after giving Lucy another big hug they sat down and enjoyed their meal.

The rest of the afternoon Lucy walked Serena around the bookstore and commended her on doing her homework and familiarizing herself with the layout. They discussed some upcoming book signing events, and Serena shared with Lucy some more improvement ideas she had floating around in her head. Serena was very impressed at Lucy's bookkeeping skills. Both daily activity logs for the coffee shop and bookstore were up to date and she was amazed at the income the little shop brought in.

Lucy also filled her in on the neighborhood gossip, shared with her who's who, and told some interesting facts about some of the regulars. All and all it had been a good day, but at three o'clock they called it quits. Serena was going into data overload and Lucy needed to pick up the boys. She was happy to retire to her apartment for some needed downtime. After a glass of wine, making an appointment with the security company, checking her emails and voicemails she was ready for the evening.

Serena called her sister and was so happy to hear her voice. She filled her in on the last two days, leaving out most of the details regarding Cliff. She and James spent more time researching, but every road seemed to lead to a dead end. She told him not to worry, that later this week she would call her friend Rosie. She was sure to have more of an insight into this situation since she dabbled a little in the spirit world. Upon picking up the book to put it in the living room, Serena noticed the entire title for the first time. "Hmm," Serena said as she read it out load. "Trust in others, Honor your family and Obey your heart!" She had thought the name of the book was just Trust, Honor, and Obey, the rest was printed is such small print that it was easy to miss at first glance. Serena opened the book and skimmed through the pages. This felt odd to her like she was invading James's personal space. She pondered the thought for a minute and wondered if that was even possible. She was clueless of the rules in the spirit world. The book itself did intrigue her but she would have to read it later. She felt uncomfortable reading it while James was bonded to it.   Her eyes were tired and her brain was drained. Serena placed the book on the living room end table and retired herself to the night, hoping that some special tall handsome man would come fulfill her fantasies in her dreams.

Serena followed the same pattern through the rest of the week.   Each day she became more familiar with the bookstore. She made coffees, assisted customers and even learned how to operate the cash registers with confidence. Hopefully, it would only be temporary because the new cash registers were due in next week.   Lucy had introduced her to some of the regulars and Serena laughed as she noticed some of the quirks Lucy had shared with her.   By the end of the week, she was feeling so confident about handling the shop that Serena gave Lucy some time off. She felt safe now that she had a top of the line security system installed. She still wondered who those people were and why they wanted the book. At any means, they were not going to be able to get back into the store during non-business hours, and that was perfectly fine with her. She had tried to push the couple out of her mind but she did catch herself being overly cautious a time or two, checking out the customers looking for anything suspicious.

Cliff had called a couple times during the week and Serena was surprised to find that she looked forward to his calls. It was easy to talk to him, and she enjoyed listening as he talked about his day and all of Brody's funny moments. On Thursday, Cliff informed her of a job he had to do out of town. Hearing that, Serena felt a little pang of sadness but instead of dwelling on that thought, she decided it would be the perfect weekend to head over to Seaside and visit with her friend Rosie. So she made a quick call to her and it turned out that Rosie was free, and would love to have Serena for the weekend.

Friday night as Serena was packing, James, who seemed to be quiet most days, spoke up. "How long are you going to be gone?" he asked with concern in his tone.

"Just Saturday, I should be back early in the evening on Sunday. Why are you going to miss me?" Serena teased.

"Could be, I just have gotten used to having someone around that can hear me and that I can talk to. It's going to be a little lonely around here without you," James admitted.

Serena, who had formed a bond to the spirit, felt bad and wanted so much to help set him free. "I'll be back before you know it and hopefully with some answers on how to help you, or, at least, know where to start looking," Serena said, hoping that she wasn't giving James false hope. "I am going to put the book in the closet and lock the bedroom and apartment doors. Nobody should be able to get in now that we had an updated security system, but I am still going to take extra precautions."

"Thanks again Serena," James replied with a hint of compassion in his voice. "I wish that I was real so I could hug you and show my appreciation for everything you have done for me."

"That's so sweet; just knowing that you would if you were able touches my heart. I just wish that I could do more." Maybe this weekend, Serena thought, crossing her fingers for good luck.

11) A FRIENDLY VISIT

Saturday morning, Serena stepped into her shower and lavished in the warm spray hitting her skin. She was so happy that Cliff had been able to fix it so soon. As he briefly passed through her mind she wondered what he was doing and if he was thinking about her too. Hopefully, he would call her later, but she couldn't expect him to. It wasn't like they were together. They were just friends with a strong attraction to one another. You just keep telling yourself that, Serena said to herself.

Hair done, dressed in Jeans, short boots and a light green pullover, Serena loaded up her car, set the alarm, and made sure the doors were securely locked, then headed south. Seaside was only a forty minute drive and the weather was perfect, partially sunny and very few clouds. There was a light chill in the air, as the coast did tend to be on the cooler side. Serena realized she'd probably need to add some warmer clothes to her wardrobe, especially now that she had decided to reside in Astoria. She was sure she wouldn't have trouble talking Tess into another shopping trip. Thinking about her sister brought a smile to her face. She couldn't wait to see her family on Wednesday for her weekly visit to Portland. Right now she was looking forward to spending some girl time with Rosie; it had been over a year since they had gotten together and their visit was long overdue.

As Cliff headed to Florence to build a fence for a couple's retirement house, he found his thoughts wandering to the last few days he'd spent with Serena. In fact, she seemed to be with him most of his waking hours, and sometimes late at night, she appeared in his dreams. Even though he wanted to lay her down and take her body, he also felt something much deeper. He loved the way her teasing and sassy humor came out when she let down her guard. Cliff had never met anyone quite like her and he knew he was developing strong feelings for the sweet redhead. Could it be love he wondered?

Normally on his long drives, Cliff would shut down and enjoy this time. He would lay his seat back and turn up the tunes, while Brody found the open window and happily embraced the wind. Then both man and dog would cruise and chill. But not this time. Cliff was having a hard time putting Serena out of his mind, especially when vivid images of her standing naked in his shower, kept popping up in his head.

Serena arrived that morning at Rosie's shop close to Ten The closed sign was still lit up and below it, the business hours were plainly marked. "Open 10:00 to 5:00 Monday through Friday and if I am not out of town then 11:00 to 3:00 on Saturday; Sunday closed." Rosie had told Serena she would be there and that was confirmed by her sporty little Beamer convertible parked around back.

Serena admired the overflowing flower boxes filled with a

beautiful assortment of colorful flowers on her front porch and a large sign in the front that said it all. 'Rosie's Healing House. All are welcome'.

Upon entering the little store Serena was pleasantly assaulted with the fusion of herbs, incense, and light smelling candles. It immediately pulled her into as state of calming bliss. Maybe she should think about creating a little space in her store to carry some of these items. It would be a good addition to her inventory, and as a bonus it would make her store smell good.

Rosie was lounging, by the front desk reading a magazine about herbs and gardens when Serena walked in. As usual, she was dressed in the latest styles looking as beautiful as ever. Standing 5'4 in her precious petite frame, it was easy to see God had gifted her with all the right curves in all the right places. Her soft long dark chocolate hair was resting on her left shoulder. Born and raised in Africa, she had been blessed with the most beautiful sun kissed skin that was a perfect contrast to her big brown eyes. The beauty she so exuded on the outside was as much threaded throughout the inside. This you could plainly see when her face lit up as she offered you a smile.

After the two women gave long overdue hugs, they sat at a little table at the back of the shop enjoying a cup of freshly made chamomile tea. Serena relaxed, enjoying herself as Rosie gave her a quick update of her life.

As Serena listened to her friend she couldn't help but sense a little sadness in her voice. Of course, a person wouldn't know the pain that has caused it because she buried it down deep, but Serena knew because of their close friendship. Rosie had met a wonderful man, Devin, while attending college, and they were married shortly after graduation. Five years later Devin was in a terrible car accident and died in the hospital. Serena knew Rosie was still hurting, they had been soul mates and best friend; and the day he died a part of Rosie died along side of him. It destroyed her inside, she never got the chance to say goodbye. After months of grieving and isolating herself, she decided, out of protest, to move on with her life. She bought the shop and worked day and night to make it a successful business.

Besides working the shop, Rosie took on other responsibilities to keep her busy. She taught an exercise class once a week, spent hours working in her gardens and on some weekends led trail tours throughout the Oregon coast. Despite the fact that she kept herself so busy and her time was full and rewarding, Serena knew there was a deep hole in her soul that haunted her friend. Serena could understand the pain as she too had experienced losing someone she loved, but not to the degree that Rosie had suffered. What saddened Serena the most was that Rosie vowed never to fall in love again. She confessed to Serena that there would never be anyone like Devin. She also admitted she was afraid to love a man again, only to have him taken away from her. She couldn't walk through that pain ever again. Serena hoped that someday she would change her mind.

The girls got a chance to talk briefly in-between helping customers. This time, Serena took the floor and shared briefly about Cliff and James, but didn't go into detail with either man in her life. She was going to save that for later. She focused more on visiting and keeping things light.

Around noon, Rosie hung her Out-to-Lunch sign on the door and showed Serena her thriving organic herb garden. Walking out into the greenhouse in back of the store was like walking into a gourmet kitchen. Serena's nose started dancing as it was seduced by the heavenly scents permeating from the little room. She was in awe at the rows and rows of little plants, arranged by category, sitting side by side. Serena wasn't familiar with all of them ,but she knew that they provided a role in the healing realm.

Rosie closed her shop an hour early so she could spend quality time with Serena. After she served her last customer, she quickly balanced the till, locked up her shop and escorted Serena to her house by the beach.

Pulling into the driveway, surrounded by a white picket fence, sat a small but quaint little cottage. It was painted in white and sky blue, and paired together with a single car garage in like colors.

Serena grabbed her overnight bag out of the car, and as she walked up to the porch, she took in the yard. It painted a postcard picture as the lavender clematises stretched their vines up to kiss the clouds, and the red and white angelic rose bushes, graced the grounds. Adding to the masterpiece was a garden filled with a variety of wildflowers, which moved gently in the light coastal breeze. After being engulfed by the beauty of the yard, singing wind chimes welcomed you onto the porch with their magical soft voices. Looking off the porch Serena watched as Rosie retrieved her belongings from her car, and she couldn't help to feel a pang of envy wrapped in a little sadness. What she wouldn't give to have a house and a yard that was all hers, a place she could call home? She had been so close, Kevin and her had talked on many occasions about buying a house. They would usually get into silly debates over the difference in their designing styles. She took a deep breath to steady her breathing and thought to herself, Kevin didn't get to spend any time in her head, so closing that door, she moved on.

As Serena followed Rosie into the house a pleasant mixture of honeysuckle and cinnamon filled the air. She took in her surroundings. The living room décor was perfectly done is just the right blend of teal, tan and brown tones and a small splash of pink. Serena was especially fond of the cathedral ceiling and terracotta floors which lent a Caribbean feel. A matching sofa and love seat offered a comfortable place to sit, and for your reading enjoyment, garden magazines lay fanned out on an oak table. A bookshelf, also in oak, held all Rosie's health and healing books and in the corner sat a woodstove ready to rescue you from a chilly night. Of course, no home would be complete without the flat screen.

"I just love this room," Serena said, admiring her friend's decorating style. "You redecorated since the last time I was here. I really like the seascape pictures," Serena commented, motioning to the paintings on the wall.

Rosie, taking their coats to the closet turned and replied, "Yes, I did. It needed a makeover just like my life. The plain brown and tans were depressing not to mention, boring and dull."

Serena smiled at her friend. "You succeeded; this home definitely breathes a happy environment.."

"That's what I was aiming for," Rosie said, motioning Serena to follow her down the hall. "My good days finally outnumber the bad ones, but a hard one will creep in on occasion. I wanted to come home to a place that was cheerful, in hopes that I could alter my mood and pull myself back into the present." Rosie stopped and opened the door to an adorable little guest bedroom, complete with a double bed, dresser and a white wicker chair. "This is your room for tonight, I hope you like it," Rosie said as she walked over to close the blinds.

Serena plopped herself down on the bed and stared up at her friend. "What's not to like, it's perfect and this bed is so comfortable." Serena said, stretching out her legs. "Do you have a special herb to bless the bed and ensure hot steamy dreams?" Serena giggled.

Rosie laughed at Serena's quirky comment; she had forgotten how good it was to almost feel normal and was happy to have this time to spend with her best friend. "I'll see what I can find," she answered with a wink. "I'll let you get comfortable, there's a little adjoining bathroom if you want a shower or freshen up," she stated, pointing to a door next to the dresser. "I'm going to go start dinner. See you in a few." Rosie said, walking out of the room.

Serena lay across the bed wondering what Cliff was doing, and without hesitation, got out her phone and texted him;

"Hi" followed by a couple smiley faces, then went out to join Rosie in the kitchen.

Cliff, just finishing up for the day, smiled when he saw he had a message from Serena. Calling his trusty dog to his side, he snapped a selfie of them and replied, *"Hi back at* ya! *Hope you are having a fun time."* and attached a smiley face. Then Cliff motioned to Brody to hop up in the cab of the truck, loaded up his tools and headed back to his hotel room. He was going to clean up and get at bite to eat. It has been a busy day and as tired as he was, he had a feeling it was going to be an early night. He still had additional work to do on the fence, and was hoping to leave around two tomorrow afternoon. To make that happen, he would need to get a fairly early start in the morning.

While the girls dined on a delicious chicken veggie salad Serena told her about James and the strange connection she had with him.

Rosie listened closely as Serena shared her story. After her friend was done, she expressed to Serena her own thoughts on this matter. "From what you have told me it sounds like a love/hate spell. Whoever did this was hurt and feeling betrayed. The combinations of these two emotions linked so strongly together, would allow this spirit to be bonded so tightly to the book. Chances are, they had some powerful Wiccan prepare the spell or create a liquid potion."

"Is there anything that can be done to unbind him and set him free?" Serena asked, hoping her friend had the magic answer.

"Hmm, let me think," Rosie said, pondering the thought with careful attention, as her long nails tapped on the table. "Well," she stated, "first you need to find out who cast the spell and why."

Serena, taking a sip from her wine, gave her friend the deer in the headlights look, before responding. "How am I supposed to do that? I don't know any witches or where to even begin to look. It's not something in my everyday need to know list. I don't suppose I can Google it?"

Rosie laughed at her friend. "No, you can't Google it. You may not realize it Serena but witches walk among us every day. Although they prefer to be called Wiccans, they are regular people that mostly keep to themselves and practice a little magic. They don't wear pointed hats, carry around brooms and have green skin or warts on their noses. They look normal, just as we do," Rosie said as she cleared the table and topped off their glasses. "Let's go into the living room and see what I have that might lead you in the right direction."

Walking over to the bookshelf Rosie retrieved a large notebook and pulled a piece of paper out of it. She took a highlighter from a container holding pens and pencils and marked some specific areas, then brought it over to Serena. "Here is a list of shops in your surrounding area that are owned or managed by people who might be able to help you. I highlighted the ones that are likely to know of this form of spell."

Serena studied the paper, not too thrilled by the idea of going to any of these places, replied with a crack in her voice, "You want me to do what? I don't think so."

Rosie watched her friend's reaction. She herself wouldn't have a problem with going to any of those places. It was obvious that Serena would, as she stood starring down at the paper with her mouth wide open and eyes bulging. Rosie could sense that what she was instructing her friend to do was certainly out of her comfort zone. Rosie was, however, very curious how this was all going to play out. Little city girl meets coastal Wiccan, she thought smiling inside.

Serena still in a mild shock, looked up at Rosie and asked in a pleading voice. "Please tell me there is another way – I wouldn't even begin to know what to say," Serena paused, taking a large gulp of wine. Maybe she could get lost in the alcohol and forget this conversation ever happened. But her big mouth had made a promise to James and she was always good on her word. Idiot, Idiot, Idiot! She chanted.

"I can't very well go in there and ask, hi have you heard of any good spells lately, like maybe one that would keep a spirit trapped in a book," Serena said in a sarcastic tone as she walked over to the sofa and sat down. Then curling her legs underneath her, she tried to relax. "If you haven't noticed, doing this scares me a little, no, more than a little." She remarked to Rosie, who had made herself comfortable in an oversized chair.

"Serena, there is nothing to worry about," Rosie said, showing a teasing smile. "Do you think that they might put a spell on you?" She giggled.

"Nooooo of course not," Serena replied, hoping she sounded more convincing to Rosie than to herself because that thought had been in the forefront of her mind.

"Good!" Rosie said. "I know most of the owners and they don't usually go around casting spells on people on a routine basis. But just in case, how do you look in green, say a toad color?" She giggled again.

Serena threw Rosie a fake smile along with a little throw pillow sitting next to her. "That was totally not funny girlfriend!"

The girls both laughed as they talked about how crazy this conversation had gone. Rosie offered to go into the shops if she could, or at least call and give them a heads up. This seemed to lift Serena's spirits and the strange burden off of her shoulders.

Moving past that horrible task, Serena asked Rosie something that had been weighing heavily on her mind. "There is still something that bothers me. Do you know why I can hear James and nobody else can?" she asked her friend.

Rosie pondered that thought for a moment. After taking a sip of her wine, she answered. "I don't know the answer to that, but if I were to speculate, I would say that your kindred spirit, is somehow linked together. You did say that the spell mentioned something about him helping someone find love, and that would be the key to his freedom. Maybe it was a coincidence, or the universe put you there to help one another."

Serena deliberated on her girlfriend's theory. James had said it might be her, but at the time she was not interested in any relationships. She felt different now. Was she in love with Cliff? If so, how did that have anything to do with freeing James? There were so many unanswered questions. At least, Rosie had given her a list of places that might help her.

"Serena," Rosie said, pulling Serena out of her thought. "Is it possible you could be falling in love with this Cliff guy?"

"Funny, I was just asking myself that same question. I guess it could be a possibility. I enjoy being with him, he makes me laugh and treats me with kindness and respect. He is quite handsome, a damn good kisser and has a hot bod." Serena confessed to her friend, feeling her cheeks flush.

"Well," Rosie commented. "Looking at the gleam in your eyes and ditsy smile on your face when you talk about him, I would say it was a strong possibility."

To be honest with you Rosie, it really scares me to put myself out there and risk being hurt again, but at the same time, I don't want to lose him," Serena strongly stated, wrapping her arms around a throw pillow and holding it tight against her for added security.

Rosie who was taking a mental walk in the past, nodded, then replied, "I understand totally how you feel. It isn't easy starting over, you find yourself second guessing every move. It seems like every emotion is fighting against one another trying to find a balanced ground," Rosie remarked, closing her eyes and laying her head back in the chair as she meditated on the moment.

"Have you given any thought about wanting to find love again?" Serena said, thinking this would be a good time to pose the question.

Rosie thought hard about the question Serena had asked and was torn on how to answer her. She had battled with this exact same thing and still didn't know what she wanted. After a heavy sigh, Rosie looked at her friend and answered, "I don't know. Sometimes I do get very lonely and miss having a man around. Other times, I don't give it a second thought. He would have to be willing to accept my life with no expectations and I would have to do the same with his. Not sure I'm ready for that or ever will be."

Serena smiled at her friend and expressed, "We sure are a sappy pair aren't we."

"We sure are!" Rosie smiled back in agreement.

"Well, I don't know about you but this sappy girl is wiped," Serena stated with a yawn.

"I am with you girl, it's been a long day. I'm so glad you came down. We need to get together more often," Rosie expressed, as she picked up their empty glasses.

"I am glad too, I miss our girl time. You're right, and no more excuses," Serena said with another yawn as she followed Rosie into the kitchen. Then after they said goodnight, they headed for bed. Before Serena went to sleep, she checked her cell phone and was excited to see a reply from Cliff with the attached picture. She blew them both an air kiss, plugged in her phone and shortly after that she fell asleep.

The next morning Serena had awoken refreshed. In fact, she couldn't remember the last time she had slept so sound. She also laid there for a minute as the flashback of the dream she had, came to her mind. It had been about Cliff, she couldn't remember all the details but the pieces she could recollect made her tingle, releasing as a wave of desire that shot through her. She wondered if her subconscious conjured up the dream, or if Rosie was responsible for her fantasy encounter. Maybe it was a little of both. At that thought, she rose to start her day.

She found Rosie up and dressed in her running clothes standing in the kitchen with a giant cup of coffee and bagel in her hand. After good mornings, Serena helped herself to a large coffee and instead of a bagel she chose a banana from the fruit bowl, nicely displayed on the counter. Then they convened to the patio to take in the morning sun and enjoy a little girl time before they started the day.

By three that day, the girls were exhausted; they had definitely used every hour given to them wisely. The day had started with a long run on the beach, and after they cleaned up and grabbed a bite to eat, they headed to the heart of downtown Seaside to check out the boutiques in the shopping mall. After that, it was on to the outlet mall where Serena found a couple new pairs of jeans. Recently she had noticed hers were getting a little big and she was ecstatic to find out, she had moved down a size. If anything, this move had caused her to change her eating habits and get more exercise. Running on the beach was the best exercise and it was so invigorating.

At four, back at the house, they ate leftover chicken salad from last night and talked about when they could meet up again. As much as Serena was excited to get back home, she also didn't look forward to saying goodbye to Rosie. At least, she lived a lot closer now and could visit her more often. Finally after hugs and mini-conversations that kept holding her there, Serena left her friend and headed home. The weatherman had reported early evening fog and she hoped that she could make it home before it arrived.

Driving down the road, rocking out to her 80's CD, Serena was startled when she heard a loud thump. Then all of a sudden her smooth riding Subaru started a series of thump, thump, thump, thump. Serena took a firm grasp on the steering wheel and directed the vehicle safely to the side of the road. Loosening her grip on the steering wheel, she laid her head down. "A flat tire, really I can't believe this." She shrieked as she vented out loud to nobody in particular. After her little mental breakdown, Serena cautiously got out to access the damage. The right rear tire was flat and the fog was closing in. She knew how to change a tire but that's what she had Triple A for. Besides, it scared the crap out of her being on the highway alone. There were so many crazy people in this world and any number of them could be driving down Highway 101. She felt like a sitting target. Feeling very vulnerable and not fond of becoming a statistic, she hurried back into the car, locked the doors and frantically proceeded to dig in her purse for her Triple A card.

While she was desperately looking for her card, Serena was startled by a tap at her window, The next moments happened so fast for her, scared to death, Serena reacted without thinking. Panic stricken adrenalin poured out of her. Before the assailant could identify themselves she released the pepper spray she had grabbed out of her purse, and sprayed it through the partially rolled down window, right into their eyes.

A very upset person started yelling out some profane words, and as she listened to the voice, it occurred to her she had a pretty good idea who it belonged to.

12) PLAYING IT SAFE

Serena peeked out the window to get a closer look. It was hard to see clearly in the dark, which was laced with a light coat of misty fog. She was hoping she was wrong but her suspicion was rightly confirmed. Yep, that man dancing around, hands plastered to his face, still yelling out some very choice words, was Cliff. "Oh my goodness, Serena said in a whisper, I just half-blinded him with pepper spray, that's not a good thing." She knew from her first aid training that she had to get the spray off him immediately. So for a temporary solution, until she could get him home, she dabbed a paper towel with water from her bottle and opened the door carefully. He didn't seem very happy at the moment which was very understandable. Serena could imagine how it must sting.

Cliff who had found Serena alongside the road, stopped to see if everything was okay. Getting out of his truck he noticed the rear flat tire and saw her sitting in her car. He quietly walked up to the driver side, to not alarm her and gently tapped on the window. The next thing he knew his eyes were burning like there was a fire blazing in them. He then felt Serena work to pry his hands from his face and place a cool towel on his eyes. Then she repeated over and over how sorry she was. This cool wet touch of the towel seemed to sooth the burning sensation but only to a small degree.

"Please tell me you didn't just spray me with mace?" Cliff asked, standing there looking quite pathetic with his eyes squinting and wiping his runny nose.

Serena, trying to wipe Cliff's eyes while dealing with his flapping hands and sporadic coughing attacks, answered, "No, it was pepper spray." Trying to keep the mood light she added. "Well, the good news is that only a little spray got through the crack in the window. The bad news is that the burning may last for a while. Oh, Cliff, I am so sorry."

"Please stop saying you're sorry!" Cliff said in a rough voice, with a little twinge of anger. "I would just like to know something, though. Why in God's creation did you spray me?" he asked, trying to keep his anger at bay.

Serena was trying not to let Cliff's anger get to her; she knew it wasn't personal and in his predicament she would probably do the same. So dismissing his actions, she answered back. "I let fear get the best of me, I started thinking about everything that could happen to me being alone and stranded on this highway. If that wasn't bad enough, to add to my fragile nerves, it was starting to get dark and foggy. The tap on the window startled me. My self-defense training taught me to act first and ask questions later and that's what I did.   Maybe you should've called me," Serena added, clenching her teeth and raising her shoulders, still in shock over what she had done.

Cliff was thinking to himself, maybe he should've just kept driving. But he knew he didn't mean that, he was irritated, tired and his eyes burnt like hell. This was a combination for a nasty attitude.

"Cliff honey," Serena said calmly and softly.   "You can't drive. I am going to take you home and treat your eyes and skin. Can you call someone to get your truck?"

"I could call my friend Matt but I can't see, which makes it a little difficult to find the number on my phone," Cliff answered with a bite of sarcasm in his tone.

Cliff's sharpness stung a little but Serena shrugged it off. "Hand me your phone," Serena demanded, holding out her hand.

Serena called Triple A first and then Matt. Relief set in when he answered on the fourth ring. She explained the situation and in less than sixty minutes, they were on their way to Cliff's house. Matt's brother had dropped him off shortly after Triple A had left. After accessing the situation and helping Cliff into Serena's SUV, Matt climbed up into Cliff's truck, made himself comfortable, turned up the tunes and followed behind.   Which was a much happier ride compared to the SUV in front of him, as Serena, Cliff and Brody rode along in dead silence.

On the drive home, Cliff sat slouched in the passenger seat with the cloth on his eyes. Left with her own thoughts, Serena, feeling horrible after what she had done, tried to focus on something more pleasant.

She had enjoyed meeting Matt and found him polite and very good looking, though not quite as handsome as Cliff. Of course, she was biased. She did know of someone who might find Matt intriguing, though. Serena would first have to find out if he was available. She could probably ask Cliff, but after glancing over at him, she decide now was not a good time.

Back at Cliff's, Matt helped get him into the house. Brody with deep concern was close on his master's heels, he sensed something wasn't quite right with Cliff and wasn't about to leave his side. Serena gave him a loving pat. "He's going to be okay, boy." she told him softly, feeling a little guilty because she had inflicted this pain on his master. It was clear, she wasn't at the top of his good people list tonight.

Inside the house, Serena immediately got a washcloth, soaked it with cold water and handed it to Cliff, with instructions for him to hold it over his eyes while she said good-bye to his friend. She thanked Matt and walked him to the door. "I really appreciate you coming to our rescue. I only hope that I didn't interrupt any family time," Serena said, trying not to sound like she was prying.

Matt smiled and replied, "It was no problem, I was just sitting around watching the game on TV and there's no family, so no worries. I was glad I was there to help." Matt must have sensed that Serena was very upset over the incident so he gave her a big hug and offered a few kind words; "Don't beat yourself up over this, It was an accident and Cliff knows that. Someday you will probably look back and laugh."

Serena gave quick attention to Matt's comment as she played a small scenario in her mind of sharing this with Cliff someday. "*Remember that time I sprayed you with pepper spray, ha?*" Then an image of Cliff, after being sprayed appeared. Nope, this was definitely not a laughable moment. In fact, this was a memory that was meant to be burned and buried deep, very deep. She did, however, feel comfort in Matt's caring hug. Stepping away she looked up at him and trying to create a sincere smile, replied, "Thanks for your concern, you're probably right. It's been a long day and I'm tired, hopefully, tomorrow my mood will be in a happier place. Well, I had better go tend to Cliff, it was very nice meeting you and thanks again."

Goodbyes done and Matt gone, Serena leaned against the closed front door as she made a mental note to herself. Hmm, he was handsome, available, caring and a great hugger. Matt had many points in his favor and she knew the perfect girl for him. Proud of her match-making plan, she celebrated with a pat on her back then went to check on Cliff.

Within ten minutes of him holding the cloth on his eyes, the burning had subsided a bit. Cliff, who was really in no mood for conversation, fed Brody, grabbed a beer and headed upstairs. He wanted some downtime and a shower to make sure that all the spray was washed off his skin. Upon seeing Serena he yelled down to her, "I'm going to grab a shower and crash. You can have the spare room; it's across the room from mine. Make yourself at home, see you in the morning. Also, if you're wondering, I'm not mad, just exhausted and not feeling so hot." He sent Serena a semi-smile, turned away and continued up the stairs.

"Good night," replied Serena softly, as she watched Cliff walk up the stairs. She was also worn out. She and Rosie had stayed up late talking and drinking last night and before her flat tire, she had planned on going home, talking with James and chilling on the couch. But as usual, life had a way of throwing you curves, and lately Serena felt she had been traveling on many winding roads, since she had arrived in Astoria.

She walked around the house and made sure the doors were locked, retrieved her bag from the foyer and headed to the spare room. After getting ready for bed she texted Lucy. She told her what had happened and that she may be late getting to the shop tomorrow. Serena should have been asleep the minute her head hit the pillow, but the evening's events kept playing back in her mind. Poor James, he was going to wonder what had happened to her and she was also concerned about Cliff and hoped his eyes were better in the morning. Maybe she should go check on him, and at that thought; she quietly slipped out into the hall.

He had left his door cracked, a perfect invitation for Serena to peek in. In his king size bed she was relieved to see Cliff stretched out on his back and sleeping peacefully. Serena's eyes strayed to the big empty space next to him and longed to climb in beside. She told herself it was to keep an eye on him but it really was the desire to lie close to him. Besides, there was plenty of room on his bed. Grabbing a throw blanket from the chair, she laid down on the top of the comforter, snuggled up in the blanket and within minutes she was fast asleep. Oblivious to her that Mr. Fate and Miss Destiny were dealing the deck tonight and sleeping was not in the cards.

Cliff awoke in the middle of the night and was surprised to see Serena restfully sleeping next to him. Brody, hearing his master stir, with a stretch and shake was alert and standing next to the bed. Noticing his signal, Cliff put on his slippers and took Brody outside.

Business done, both man and dog headed back to the bedroom. Cliff still couldn't believe the beautiful angel lying on her side, was sharing his bed. He stood there for a minute thinking as he watched her. It had been awhile since another woman had shared his bed and if he was smart he would go sleep in the spare room. He knew this could only lead down a path he wasn't sure either of them were ready for. He just couldn't move, so intrigued by this gorgeous woman who was so close to his touch. He watched as the soft glow of the moon peering through the window cast a silhouette picture of her body, and the beams sent a prism of colors that danced on her fiery red hair. Cliff quietly gasped as he noticed the lacey strap of her nightgown slip off her shoulders. He knew, at that very moment, leaving the room was the furthest thing from his mind. Instead he slid in beside her and pulled her close, her body fitting so perfectly spooned into his. She was so soft and smelled of lavender and her sensual neck was begging to be tasted.

Serena felt Cliff's hard body wrap around her, she snuggled up close and let out a sigh of pleasure when he began to nibble on her neck. She turned to face him and when their lips met, two souls who had been denying deep passion for each other, collided.

Cliff felt Serena tense up, he was sure she was scared of letting go and getting hurt again. So he whispered softly in her ear. "It's okay baby, there is nothing to fear, just relax and trust me. I promise I won't hurt you."

Cliff's endearing words helped to calm Serena's fears and without another thought, she put her bruised heart into trustful hands and completely let go.

They knew no boundaries as unleashed passion and desire consumed the lovers. Their bodies longed to feel flesh on flesh as greedy hands discarded clothing, exposing a path to each vulnerable area. Each touch and sizzling kiss burned into the tangled bodies as they thrashed in the twisted covers. The smell of sex infused with musk and lavender filled the room. Their bodies drenched in sweat, experienced and explored the new territories, both eager to please and satisfy.

Cliff was mesmerized by the beauty of Serena, every kiss from her intoxicating lips and touch of her luscious skin increased his hunger for her. There was a fury ablaze inside of him eager to take her, but he went slowly to savor every decadent sensation. His sex pushed against her, she begged for release, she was wet and ready, but still he made her wait. His heart raced as her body trembled, tonight she belonged to him.

Serena's body shook with intense pleasure as Cliff took her. He awakened every nerve with each touch and taste. She gave into him completely as he drove her close to a tantalizing insanity, taking her over wave after surging wave. Her body exploded as each raging surge poured through her and even though she was tired and spent, she begged for more.

As the night moved on, the want and need grew stronger until all control was lost. The lovers embrace as their hungry bodies joined, making love; climbing higher and higher until finding that blissful release.

They both wanted more as they bathed in the aftermath of their lovemaking. But the pull of the night took hold of the couple as Cliff and Serena fell asleep, wrapped securely in each other arms. Somewhere across town, a voice, no one could hear, yelled out, "Hot damn!"

The next morning Serena awoke to the sight of a hairy face and big brown eyes watching her, waiting patiently for any sign of life "Good morning boy she whispered, I bet you need out. Just give me a couple minutes," she said with a yawn. All Serena wanted to do was snuggle up against the warm body next to her and let her mind drift back into the heat of last night, when the burning desire inside them was set free. Thinking about it made her body tingle. It hadn't been just sex, the man was definitely amazing in that area but there was more to it than that. Somewhere in the night Serena had felt a strong connection, something she couldn't explain. Was it love this early or lust? She wouldn't mind exploring either possibility more but right now she needed to get up. She was pretty sure Brody was in agreement with her decision as he kept gently nudging her arm with his cold wet nose. "Okay," she whispered as she attempted to slide out of Cliff's arms, but the plan backfired when he felt her slipping away, he held on to her tighter.

"Cliff honey I need to get up," Serena softly said with a yawn and tossed the covers off her to sit up.

"Stay with me!" Cliff pleaded trying to grasp tighter onto Serena, only to have her soft warm body slip through his hands. "Can't we pretend it's still yesterday and hide away from the world?" Cliff said, half begging.

Serena sitting on the bed turned and put her hand on his and replied, "As much as I would love to stay here, I have a responsibility to the store right now. Besides, I am pretty sure you wouldn't want to revisit yesterday's nightmare."

Cliff blinked and his sandpaper dry eyes were quickly in agreement with that. "Well, probably not the pepper spray adventure but the rest I wouldn't mind re-enacting," he said, running his fingers down her arm.

Serena could tell Cliffs eyes were still bothering him by the way he was squinting. She still felt bad about spraying him. With sympathetic eyes, she stated, "Oh Cliff I am….." Before she could finish her sentence Cliff gently put his

210

finger up to her lips and interrupted. "I think you broke the Guinness book of records of I'm sorry in one night,"

Gently removing his finger, she replied, "I still feel so bad," she admitted.

"Serena" stated Cliff as he pulled her close. "You didn't do it on purpose, probably better it happened to me instead of a police officer. He might have shot first and asked questions later. Let's just drop it and move on. However, If you would like to make it up to me, I think I could come up with a few ideas." He said in a sexy sleepy voice as he nuzzled her neck, causing a trail of goose bumps to travel down her spine.

"Stop it," she giggled. "You are playing dirty," she said, playfully pushing his arms away. This man was insatiable. "I need to get up. I told Lucy I would be at the shop this morning. Also, you need to take Brody out, he came to me a little while ago." At that, Cliff under protest, let Serena out of bed.

He was captivated by her beauty as he watched her walk away. Excitement he couldn't hide grew in him as he remembered how those never ending legs felt wrapped tight around him. Bringing himself to attention, Cliff decided to wait a couple minutes before getting out of bed.

"You are so beautiful, and don't tell me I must be blind or I need glasses." Cliff stated, looking at Serena with loving passionate eyes. Cliff was concerned when he noticed her critical reaction to his comment and sudden mood change. "Serena is everything alright? Did I say something wrong?

Please talk to me honey."

Serena tried to hide the sadness in her eyes as she bent down to pick up her clothes. Feeling a little vulnerable, hoping to cover herself with the pile in her hands, she turned and answered. "When Kevin and I first got together he would tell me that he loved me almost every day. Then the last few months of our relationship I think he might have said it a couple times." After pausing to take a deep breath and gather her thoughts, she continued. After he left I realized they were just useless words just like our relationship had been. "If I was so beautiful why did he want someone else?" She asked herself, holding tight to her emotions and not wanting to cry. "She must be prettier, must have a better body than me. I couldn't grasp the reasons so I guess I still feel those words are meaningless and joking about it helps to ease the sting of the pain."

Cliff taken in by Serena's openness and willing to share a very emotional pain with him, got out of bed and took her in his arms. When she looked up at him he could see the hurt and pain in her eyes. Catching a stray tear trailing down her cheek he replied. "Listen Serena," Cliff said, "he was a fool for letting you go. Besides being beautiful and I truly mean this, you are a fun, passionate, caring, and loving lady with a little sassy tied in. You can ask anyone that knows me; I don't express my feelings to many women. You are very special to me so no more thinking about that jerk, ok?"

Serena smiled and nodded her head, Cliff wrapped her face in his hands and finding her lips he sealed it with a long slow kiss then pulled away and swatted her ass. "Now go get ready or we are going back to bed and I'm keeping you as my sex hostage for the rest of the day."

Serena, blushing a little, smiled at the thought which scared her as much as it intrigued her. Looking at Cliff she knew he was serious so she headed for the bathroom. Remembering her awful experience the last time she used his shower, Serena left the door crack a little. As she proceeded to get in, Serena heard Cliff yell out, "and might I add to the list she is smart and a fast learner." That brought a smile to Serena, knowing he was referring to the unlocked door. She adjusted the shower head before she climbed into the stall and just as she turned the water on she heard Cliff call for Brody. Water flowing she stepped under the tranquil waterfall and let the spray wash away the lingering scent of Cliff from her body. She wanted so much to believe him and trust him with her heart. But a part of her was not willing to fall completely and let go. She was still very guarded.

Done with her shower and ready for the day, Serena went to the kitchen to join Cliff. He had made coffee and at the table. There were bagels, bananas, and yogurt. They shared a little small talk and kept the conversation on a surface level, neither of them were ready to talk seriously about what had happened last night. She couldn't explain it but she felt a little awkward not really knowing what to say or how to act. Was this a one-time fling? Would things go back to normal now? She wondered what Cliff was feeling or thinking and was afraid to find out. There were so many questions and so few answers. Serena wasn't sure if she was ready for another relationship, it would probably just complicate her life.

Ready to leave, Serena attempted to give Cliff a quick kiss but he had other ideas as he took her into his arms and gave her a mind blowing deep passionate kiss.

This caught Serena off guard and her un-sensible self was trying to take charge, she wanted to rip off his clothes and devour him in the foyer but damn, her sensible self stepped back in and took control. So she said goodbye and walked out the door. When Serena felt she was a safe distance away she turned and blew him a kiss. She then got in her car and quickly drove away.

Cliff watched as Serena drove away. His head was reeling as the taste of Serena lingered on his lips and the remnants of the night came to the forefront of his thoughts. He could sense she was uncomfortable this morning and in deep thought. She was a little reserved and definitely had her guard up. Cliff, himself was wondering if last night was a mistake. It certainly didn't feel like one to him. Could he see himself in a relationship with Serena?

He closed the door and headed back into the kitchen. He thought about the last few weeks and the time that they had spent together. He did miss her when she was away and he looked forward to seeing her again. The answer was "yes" he could see her in his life; in fact, he didn't want to live his life without her. But he knew that he was going to have to gain her trust and break down the walls that guarded her heart. He would also need to tell Tom which he wasn't looking forward to. He valued their friendship and Cliff wasn't sure how Tom would react. Grabbing his keys, he called Brody and they headed for work.

Lucy was on the phone when Serena walked into the shop. She gave her a little wave and decided to go upstairs and talk with James for a few minutes. She was excited to tell him what Rosie had shared with her. She still wasn't comfortable going into the shops Rosie had suggested Serena, however, worked up a plan. She would introduce herself as the new shop owner in town and offer them a $5.00 gift card for the café. That would, at least, get her foot in the door. She hadn't figured out how she would bring up the subject of James yet. That was going to take a lot more thought.

Serena went into the closet and retrieved the book. "Finally, you're home," James excitedly yelled. "I have been waiting to tell you my good news."

Serena wondered what he was so excited about. Whatever it was, had caused the spirit to be upbeat and happy. "I'm sorry," Serena apologized. It's been a long weekend and I also have some news to tell you. Serena replied, placing the book on the nightstand and plopping down on her bed.

"Me first," James said before Serena could jump in.

"Okay, okay." Serena answered, curious to hear his news as she made herself comfortable on the bed.

"Ask me who I am," James enthusiastically stated.

"Really James, is this a Joke?" Serena asked, not sure where this conversation was heading and not interested in playing games.

"Serena, please humor me," James pleaded.

Serena sighed, then giving into James request, asked. "Who are you?" She asked with a puzzled look on her face.

Then the floodgates opened.

"Let me introduce myself to you; my name is Broderick James Hallow. I was born in Astoria in 1932, I had 4 brothers, went to Piedmont High, and Eastern Oregon University for a couple years. I worked at the local mill while I studied to get my associates degree. I was engaged to Judith McAlister."

Serena interrupted, with a look of surprise she jumped in. "James; How? What? When did this happen." Serena asked. She wanted to know all about her roommate.

James continued, "It was so bizarre Serena. I was out floating through the store like usual and all of a sudden I felt this strange sensation. Then all of a sudden I started remembering dates and events. There are still some blank pages and holes I can't fill in. I hope that in time I will be able to remember everything."

Serena wondered what could have happened last night to have loosened the bind on the spell. Maybe she would ask Rosie tomorrow but right now she was curious about the life of James. "Please continue James," Serena said with urgency in her voice, making herself comfortable on her bed.

"Well, as I was saying, I was engaged and one day I was in this bookstore and there she was. The most beautiful women I have ever laid my eyes on. I believe it was your Aunt, Serena. I can remember it like it was yesterday. I was so mesmerized by her beauty and kindred spirit that I couldn't stay away. I made up excuses to my fiancée and found myself coming to the shop whenever I could get away. I even became an avid reader. Funny thing was, I didn't even like to read but it allowed me to be closer to Carol."

After pausing for a moment, James continued. "I knew what I was doing was wrong even though there was no physical relationship, there seems to be a strong emotional connection. I had never experienced those feelings with Judith. Carol made me feel so alive and I was much happier when we were together. Her smile lit up her angelic face and I could listen to her boisterous laugh all day. I started questioning my relationship with Judith and wondered if I was really in love with her. Now that I am looking back maybe we got together more for convenience instead of love. I was torn between marrying Judith or breaking our engagement and pursuing a life with Carol. She understood how I felt, and being the sweet loving person she was, Carol never pushed for a decision."

"After giving my dilemma considerable thought, I decided to break it off with Judith and start a new a life with Carol. Sadly enough, I never got the chance to tell her. After that I don't remember much, it's like there's a big black hole."

"Wow," Serena exclaimed, thinking back in time when her aunt was alive. She was a lovely lady and everything he'd said about her was true. She just couldn't understand why he kept calling her Carol, though; it must have been an enduring nickname he had given her. Serena hadn't realized how much she missed her Aunt. She could also remember her joyful laugh, it was a characteristic that was passed onto Lucy as well.

"That is great news James," commented Serena. "Now we know who you are, and I just may have a way to find out how you got into the book. Finding the answers to those key clues, will probably lead us on the path to your freedom.

James became silent as Serena proceeded to tell him her news. He hoped that another piece of the puzzle would be revealed

Serena explained to James everything that Rosie had shared, including going into the other stores. At least, she had the name of his Fiancé, Serena was pretty sure that she played a part in this twisted mess.

Serena, needing to feed her curiosity regarding an important fragile matter, directed her question to him. "Do you think it's possible that Judith is responsible for locking your spirit in the book?"

James pondered the question for a moment before answering. "Suppose it's possible, it's just hard to think that she would do such a terrible thing. I have to say she was quite angry after I told her of my decision. She had admitted to me that she had suspected something was going on and warned me that I would regret leaving her."

"Hmm..., quite interesting," commented Serena. "I would love to spend more time discussing this with you and do more research but I really need go downstairs and help out Lucy."

"Okay, I understand," James replied with a little sadness in his voice.

Serena noting his mood change commented. "James, don't sound so down. We have made considerable progress and you got most of your memory back. Hang in there." At that, Serena said goodbye to the entity and headed downstairs.

After Lucy and Serena shared a little girl time they walked through their daily Monday routines in the bookstore. There was a book signing happening next month and they made notes of everything they needed to do to prepare for it. They also took inventory to determine what needed to be ordered. After her and Lucy were finished Serena repeated the same process in the coffee shop. She tried to concentrate on ordering supplies but her mind kept wandering. Part of her was focusing on the task at hand while the other part was dancing with images of the night before. She chuckled to herself when she imagined mixing up her thoughts and ordering four gallons of naked sexy man instead of milk.

Serena attempted to concentrate on business matters. Normally she had no problem leaving her personal life outside of work. This was ridiculous, she thought. She felt like a giddy school girl with a high school crush. Maybe it was love, it felt like love. What else could it be? Upon coming to terms with this realization, Serena wasn't sure if she wanted to do the happy dance or run. She just wasn't sure if her heart was completely ready. But if it wasn't then, hopefully it would concede. She could feel a sense of peace embrace her when she thought about Cliff. This was a strong indication that maybe she was ready to let him in. At that thought she badly wanted to see him. With her mind made up, she was going to have to put her big girl panties on and tell him how she felt.

Down the street a few blocks, at the Jewelry shop, Cliff was dealing with his own emotions as he also tried to keep his mind on this work. It was imperative that he stay grounded, he had already hit his finger twice with the hammer while trying to hang drywall. He kept losing focus, it was difficult to concentrate and he was discovering he was a hazard to his body. That damn girl just wouldn't get out of his head and his thoughts were being held hostage by X-rated images of Serena. It excited him but it wasn't the place or time to be daydreaming. Last night he had seen a softer more vulnerable side of her. She moved with such deep raw passion; daringly, boldly and fearlessly. However, the next morning it was like waking up with a different person. She was shy, reserved and cautious. She was a woman of mystery for sure. There were definitely skeletons in her closet and secrets locked away, she wasn't willing to share. He would do whatever it took to peel away the layers of hurt and fear to find that woman again.

Brody's bark brought Cliff back to the surface, he was informing Cliff he needed out and that it was probably time for a treat. "Okay boy," Cliff said to his trusty companion. "Hang in there for a few more minutes and we'll go for a quick walk." Afterwards, he would need to put himself into fourth gear and get moving on this remodel. He had a deadline and intended on meeting it. He would have to put his thoughts of Serena aside, maybe blast her out of his mind with some loud rock music. If only it was that simple.

Meanwhile, back at Books on the Corner Serena had made a decision to go to Cliff and she went off to find Lucy to let her know. Lucy was in the romance section organizing the authors in alphabetical order. It seemed to be an ongoing task. "Hey Luce, you think you can handle things here for about an hour? I am going to run a coffee over to Cliff. He is working a couple blocks away, remodeling Johns Gems."

"Sure, no problem," answered Lucy with an extra pronounced smile on her face. "I do have a few more things I would like to accomplish today so take your time. If you're not back before I am ready to leave. I will lock up and set the alarm."

"What are you grinning about?" Serena said, giving notice to the smile plastered on Lucy's face.

"Oh, nothing much, just noticing you have a little more spark in your eyes, perk in your step and glow in your skin." Lucy admitted.

"Is it that noticeable?" Serena asked.

"Well," Lucy teased. "The only thing missing is a flashing lighted sign hanging around your neck, saying 'I got laid.'"

Serena blushed at that comment. "Lucy!" she softly yelled. "Really…" She added, and then both ladies busted out laughing. One of the many things that Serena admired about Lucy was that she wasn't afraid to voice her opinion. No matter how blunt it was.

"He makes me so happy!" Serena said, spinning around with excitement. Pulling her crazy self together she and Lucy ventured to the coffee shop. They talked more while Serena prepared Cliffs coffee.

"I do have to admit that I am a little scared, but I am going to take it slow and see where it goes." Serena said. "Him and his crazy loveable dog are really starting to grow on me," She added with a giggle.

Lucy walked over to Serena and gave her a big hug, "I couldn't be happier for you, Cliff seems like a great guy and I love seeing your glowing spirit again. Now go take him that coffee before it gets cold."

"Thanks, Lucy," Serena said excitedly, placing a quick kiss

on her cheek. Then she grabbed her coat and headed towards the door.

It was a beautiful spring day. The warm sun playing peek-a-boo with the clouds and the presence of the light cool breeze meant Mother Nature was expressing that summer was just around the corner. Serena was enjoying her walk, her mind was so wrapped around Cliff that she didn't notice the couple following her. When she decided to take the shortcut through the alley it never occurred to her that she may be walking into danger. Only when Serena started down the quiet alley, did she hear the footsteps close behind her. She reached into her pocket and took hold of the pepper spray, praying she wouldn't have to use it and hoping it was just her imagination going into overdrive. They were probably just going the same way, Serena thought, trying not to panic. She remembered her self-defense training; never let them see or sense your fear. So she picked up her speed, put on a power posture and walked with a purpose. As much as she wanted to believe she was safe, the hairs on the back of her neck were telling her she wasn't.

13) TRAPPED

Serena kept up the fast pace and realized the footsteps were getting much closer. Before she knew it, she was lunged at from behind and was propelled forward causing her to drop the coffee, and lose the grip of the pepper spray. Surprisingly so, she didn't lose her balance. Serena turned around to see that her attackers were two in number wearing ski masks, making it impossible to make out their faces. They each took hold of an arm and forced her back up against the alley wall. Serena let out a blood-curdling scream which was quickly stifled by a large gloved hand. If only she could reach inside her pocket and grab her pepper spray, she would give these two a good dose. It would then give her a good opportunity to escape. What could they want with her? Her thoughts rambled, she didn't have her purse with her so they weren't going to get any money and she was wearing very little jewelry so she wouldn't be worth much. Then a man with a deep voice spoke to her.

"Where's the book witch?" He demanded removing his hand from her mouth. "I am warning you," he added. "If you scream I won't hesitate to tape your mouth shut. Do you understand?"

Serena nodded. Her head was reeling from the shock of

the attack as she tried to focus on what was happening. She was in the alley and her attackers had her pinned up against the wall. The question was why? Her body was shaking profusely. Taking a deep breath, she worked to calm her nerves and stabilize her accelerated pulse. Gathering by their comment about a book, she had a pretty good idea it was the same couple that had broken into her store. For some reason, unknown to her, they thought she was a witch. She had been called many things but never that. Trying to stay calm and play dumb Serena attempted to reason with them. "I am not a witch and I don't know what book you're talking about. It's obvious you have the wrong person. Now please get your hands off me and let me go."

"Quiet!" The male voice commanded. "You just want the treasure for yourself."

"Yeah, you greedy witch," the female voice added.

They were standing right next to her and Serena tried to eavesdrop as the couple whispered amongst themselves.

The woman asked; "What do we do with her now?"

The man paused for a minute and replied, "How am I supposed to know, never met a witch before."

The woman commented back; "Well we probably don't want to make her mad or she might cast us into a book, and unless it's a shopping catalog I don't want to go there."

Serena almost laughed; maybe out of shock or maybe because she was pretty sure these two weren't playing with a full deck. But never the less, she still didn't know what they were capable of so she listened as the two continued. Maybe she would learn something more about James.

The man paused again as though he was reaching for a plan. "Give me a minute I need time to think."

The woman who at this time sounded a little frustrated replied with a touch of sarcasm in her voice. "I thought there was a plan, you said don't worry you have it all under control. I knew this was wrong to begin with!"

The man, who also sounded frustrated, raised his voice at the woman. "I said I needed to think, can't you stop talking for just a few minutes?"

Serena heard the woman mumble something under her breath and she was sure it wasn't a kind reply. She thought this might be a good time for her to speak up again. "What made you think I was a witch and why is the book so important that you have me trapped in this alley?"

"As if you didn't know," answered the female voice, still holding a tight grip on Serena's arm, which by now was starting to fall asleep. "Only someone linked to magic could have put a spell on the book to keep it imprisoned in your store."

Serena thought to herself; for their sake they were lucky she wasn't or there would be two more rats scurrying around in the alley.

Serena blew out a breath, irritated with her attackers and boldly stated. "I am not a witch and why do you want a silly old book anyway?"

"Mom told us all about the treasure it beholds inside and it is in your shop and we want it, so stop playing games and give us the book." The male voice angrily demanded.

Serena wanted to know more about the treasure and how it was linked to James. As she was thinking to herself on how she could work this situation to her advantage and also how she could escape, a big brown flash of fur and teeth appeared from her right side. It didn't take her long to realize it was Brody and it was clearly obvious he was on a mission as he attempted to lunge at her attackers. The couple, frightened by the sight of the angry dog, released Serena and took off on a dead run staying one step ahead of the dog. She watched as they disappeared out of site with Brody close behind. After waiting a couple minutes to make sure they were really gone, Serena slid down the alley wall to a seated position. Closing her eyes and taking a deep breath, she stayed there locked in that that position as she waited for her heartbeat to get back normal. She hadn't realized how scared she had been. As she felt her pulse slow down, Serena opened her eyes and was surprised to see a shadowed Cliff crouching before her.

Cliff, whose heart had stopped when he had seen her pinned against the alley wall, ran behind Brody with mega force to get to Serena. He found her against the wall in a squatted position head down and arms wrapped around her knees like a terrified child. Cliff melted as she looked up at him with her tear filled eyes. He wasted no time helping her up and wrapping her in his arms, he held on to her tight to calm her trembling body. Silence bestowed upon them for a couple minutes and then Cliff spoke. "Serena honey, are you alright?" Cliff asked, with deep concern in his voice as he loosened his hold on her and wiped her eyes with his handkerchief.

Serena, who was gaining back her control and feeling a little better now that Cliff was here, answered, "Yes, I think so, I am so glad you're here. How did you know how to find me?" She asked, attempting to capture her balance as she stood on her own.

Cliff, trying to pull himself back together and untangle the knot in his stomach, took a deep breath and replied, "I was out back of the Jewelry store with Brody when I heard you scream. At the time, I didn't know it was you but Brody sensed something wasn't right, and took off in a search and rescue mode. My gut tells me that he knew it was you all along. Anyway, I ran behind him finding it hard to keep up and when I turned the corner and saw it was you up against the wall, my whole world stopped. I couldn't get to you fast enough and it seemed as though time was moving in slow motion, only it was probably a matter of seconds." Cliff, running his hands through his hair, admitted. "Serena, those were the most terrifying seconds of my entire life. Promise me you will never scare me like that again."

As Cliff spoke to her, Serena could hear the unsettled tone in his voice and could see the pain burning in his eyes. Was this love, or was she reading more into it. She stood facing him and answered. "I looked up and there you were, my prince charming coming to my rescue again. I also owe Brody a big hug and big dog bone. How did I ever get so lucky? I will try not to scare you again but, this time, I had no control over the situation."

"Okay, I will give you this one," Cliff replied, trying to lighten up the vibes surrounding them. Then after giving her a gentle kiss, he added. "Let's talk more about this later, I need to get you out of here and find my dog." Cliff took Serena's hand and escorted her out of the alley. When they were back out on the street and in the open where Serena was much safer, Cliff kissed her and left in search of Brody. They agreed that they would meet back at her store.

When Serena arrived back at her shop and saw only Brody and Cliff, she assumed that the attackers had gotten away. Serena went over to Brody who was lapping water from her outside dog dish and thanked him. "Good boy!" Serena said, bending down to give him a hug and not caring that his slobbery wet mouth was getting her wet. She stood up to find Cliff leaning against the building with his phone in his hand. Serena knew who he was about to call and she had to stop him. It would only make matter worse. Walking over to him, Serena took hold of his hand and look into his beautiful troubled eyes. "Cliff, can we please talk before you bring the police into this. Serena pleaded.

Cliff, looking at Serena, with a serious expression on his face, replied, "Serena, I was very understanding and accommodating with the break-in, but this is much more serious. My God girl, they had you held captive in the alley, there is no telling what would have happened if Brody and I hadn't shown up." Cliff paused for a moment and took a deep breath to give him time to settle his thoughts, then continued. "So tell me, what crazy reason could you possibly have this time?" Cliff asked, trading his serious face for a more puzzled one.

"Cliff, please hear me out," Serena said, taking a minute to decide how much information she wanted to divulge. Facing him she took both of his hands in hers and answered. "I wish I could tell you about the book but it's complicated and the police would think I was insane. Sometimes I question it myself." She said with a high pitched laugh. "I am pretty sure though they were the same couple that broke into the shop attempting to steal the book. I found out some very interesting information, so please just trust me on this one." Serena added as she waited for Cliff's reply.

"Serena," Cliff said letting go of her hand. He then sat down on the bench and placed his head in his hands as he tried to make sense out of this conversation. Raising his head he stared up at Serena and continued. "What is it about this book? What do the contents hold that would cause people to attack you in order to get their hands on it? Sorry, I am not buying that its 'complicated,'" he gestured with his hands forming quotation marks in the air. I have been patient long enough and had hoped you would have confided in me sooner, I deserve an explanation, especially if it puts your life in danger. I need to know what I might be fighting against. I will make a deal with you; even though it's against my better judgment, I won't call the police now but that's only if you agree to tell me about the book." Cliff stated as he waited for Serena's reply.

Serena walked over to the outside faucet and refilled the water dish as she pondered on what to say. She knew that Cliff was right. She had planned on telling him but not this soon. Funny thing, she thought, the universe was never timely. "I will tell you," Serena answered. "But you have to promise me two things; one, you'll keep an open mind and two; you'll listen without forming the opinion that I'm crazy. Also, after the morning I have had, I would like to continue this discussion later tonight." Serena said crossing her fingers and hoping he would agree to her request. She needed some time to process and figure out how she would present the news to him.

Even though the curiosity cat was pawing at Cliff, he could tell that the day's events had taken a toll on Serena. She looked a little weary and tired, so he agreed to give her time to rest. Besides, he had to get back to work and finish up his day. He had waited this long, a little longer wasn't going to kill him. "Tonight is fine," replied Cliff. "I still have things to take care of at work. How about if I come back around six thirty tonight? Will that give you enough time?" He asked.

Serena, thankful Cliff was giving her some time, but still not happy with the night ahead, answered. "Six thirty works, I will order some Pizza, and could you please stop and get some beer on your way over?" *You are going to need it.* A silent thought bubble formed in her head.

"Yeah, I guess I can handle that, sounds like a date. I was hoping our first date would be something a little more lavish; you deserve more of a wine and dine venue." Cliff replied with a sexy smile.

"I will look forward to that on our second date then," Serena answered. For sure this was going to be one strange date for sure, Cliff, Serena and spirit makes three. Well, it was a nice short lived relationship while it lasted. Certainly after tonight, she'd be single again.

After goodbyes Serena stepped inside the store, closed the door and leaned back against it, she definitely needed a moment or two to regroup. Welcome to my crazy life, she thought.

Serena was relieved that Lucy was not in the main shop, she was probably doing paperwork in the office. There was no reason to tell her about the incident, she would only worry and ask questions and Serena didn't want to go there, not today anyway. She was still struggling with the thought of telling her, she'd wait to see how it went with Cliff tonight.

Stretching her arms, Serena felt a slight pain in her shoulders. It was a haunting reminder of the attack in the alley. She was definitely in need of some down time. But first, she was going upstairs to take a shower. Serena stripped out of her clothes and climbed into the hot water. She felt dirty after leaning up against the alley wall and thinking about strangers hands touching her made her skin crawl. She couldn't wash away the memory but she could cleanse her body of the germs and dirt that were invading her skin. That alone would give her some peace of mind. A shiver escaped her at the snapshot image of that passed through her head but she quickly shook it off and pushed the image aside. Feeling much better, she slipped on her lazy day clothes and went downstairs to fix a good strong cup of coffee and then chill awhile on the sofa in the children's corner. On her way to the coffee shop, she passed by the office and just as she had expected, Lucy was in there and seemed to be deep in concentration. Serena, not wanting to disturb her, waved and quietly walked by.

Coffee in hand Serena made herself comfortable on the sofa. Lying with her head against the soft pillow she went over in her head all the excitement of the day. She couldn't believe she had finally agreed to tell Cliff about James. She really had no choice, how else could she explain all the strange events centered on the book. One good thing that would result in her telling Cliff is that she would have someone to talk to about James. That, of course, depended on tonight's outcome. If she could convince Cliff that there was a spirit in the book maybe he would help her look for the answers. But on the other hand, he may go running and screaming out of her door and her life forever.

Serena thought to herself on how she would tell him, wrestling with many scenarios going through her mind she played each one out. But it didn't matter because none of them sounded believable. Maybe this one she whispered to herself; "Cliff, meet your Uncle James just overlook the fact that he may look like a book but his spirit is trapped inside. Funny thing is I am the only one that can hear him." Hearing it out loud Serena decided on another option; "Cliff, now promise not to freak out, remember to keep an open mind. In this book I have here, is a trapped spirit. I know it seems crazy, imagine how I felt the first time it talked to me. Anyway, I have a strong feeling that it may be a relative of yours." Not much better Serena thought. No matter what she said, she was still going to sound like a nut case.   Serena decided to close the subject for a few minutes and try and clear the cobwebs in her head. She took a drink of her coffee and set her cup on the table, only expecting to close her eyes for a couple minutes.

The next thing Serena knew, Lucy was waking her to say goodbye. The morning must have affected her more than she realized. She tried to shake off the grogginess as she slowly pulled herself up off the couch and walked with Lucy to the door. Hugs and goodbyes done, she shut and locked it then headed upstairs to freshen up and talk with James for a bit. Maybe he had some suggestions.

Back at her apartment, Serena sat on her bed next to the book, talking to it as though it was alive. In her mind, it had taken on a presence in her life. It didn't seem that strange to her anymore, maybe she should question her sanity but after tonight, Cliff may be doing that for her.

James listened as Serena shared with him her eventful day in the alley and the news she had learned from the couple. The spirit should have been happy that he might be getting closer to freedom, but not at the expense of Serena's safety. It was never his intent to bring any harm to this sweet girl. She had shown him nothing but kindness and didn't deserve any of this.   He was so grateful because as luck would have it Cliff saved the day again. James was glad that Serena had decided to tell Cliff about him. He felt relieved that the revelation of his being could bring a strong connection between Cliff and Serena. It gave him a sense of peace knowing that Cliff would be around more and able to protect her. Since James, in his spirit form, was just a useless book that couldn't help a fly. James, of course, would never reveal this to Serena because she valued her independence and became angry when it was challenged. At any means, the night ahead would prove to be interesting as the excitement brewed within the entity at the thought of meeting his Nephew.

Serena also questioned James about a treasure but he wasn't aware of any map or reference to it in the book and he should know he had been through it way too many times. "You are welcome to look for yourself if you would like," offered James.

Picking up the book Serena felt a little uncomfortable again like she was invading his space or something. James giggled as Serena thumbed through the pages looking for a paper, napkins or anything that might resemble a map. The noise startled her which caused her to drop the book. James broke out in a roar of laughter.

"James!" Serena snapped. "That wasn't very funny, remember paybacks are a bummer." Then she picked up the book and placed it on the nightstand by the bed with a little more force than needed.

James stopped laughing and replied, "Loosen up Serena, seesh. I was just trying to take your mind off tonight. I could sense some tension in the air."

"You just startled me. I have to admit it was pretty cute," Serena admitted. Resting against the headboard of the bed Serena let out a deep sigh. "You're right, I do have a lot on my mind and I am sorry for snapping at you." Serena said, apologizing to the spirit.

"Speaking about tonight, I don't suppose you have any ideas on how to spring the news to Cliff?" Serena asked hopefully.

James thought for a few, but couldn't come up with a sound plan and every idea sounded more outlandish than the last. Serena decided it was not worth worrying about anymore and maybe the words would magically come to her. Yeah, that was going to happen, she thought. "I guess we'll just have to wing it and see where it goes, it's all I can do," Serena said, shrugging her shoulders as she gave in to her decision. "Now if you excuse me I need to get ready for tonight, Cliff will be here soon."

Serena was trying to stay focused on the night ahead but the image of her in the alley kept popping into her mind. Maybe she could push the memory back with a beer or two. It might also help to loosen her up, and the words she was looking for to tell Cliff, would miraculously appear in her head. If not she would be a little too blitz to care. Serena gave attention to the last thought, she had never been much of a drinker, an occasional beer or a glass of wine now and then was her mantra. She only gave herself permission to go past her limit on certain occasions, such as nursing a broken heart, dealing with the supernatural or being attacked in an alley. She felt they were all justifiable reasons. After excusing herself from James, Serena went to prepare for the evening.

Up on the hill at his place, Cliff was tossing the ball for Brody as thoughts of the morning played havoc on his mind. He still couldn't shake the feeling of rage that consumed him when he realized it was Serena in the alley. Those were unnerving feelings, to say the least, never before had he experienced anything like them. "Boy," Cliff called to the excited dog as he picked up the ball, but before tossing it, he bent down and hugged his companion. "'Thanks, pal, for the act of heroism you have shown today, I know you love her too." Cliff said, coming to the realization that he was really falling in love with that crazy redhead. His true feelings for Serena surfaced when he'd seen her in the alley. Yes, He was in love with Serena. The deep down, raise a family, grow old together kind of love. Cliff stood up and tossed the ball for Brody one last time. He needed to get ready. Brody caught the ball and under protest, surrendered it and went in with his master.

Inside, after Cliff showered and dressed, he sat on the couch, Brody's head in his lap, His mind reeling over the revelation of being in love and still trying to adjust and come to terms with it. Looking down at Brody, he asked. "Hey pal, you think Serena has feelings for us too?" Cliff didn't know how much his companion really understood but when he spoke to him, Brody usually answered with a tail wag or a raised ear, and that was enough for Cliff. "I don't want to say too much too early and take a chance of frightening her off, so maybe we should keep it low key for a while. What do you say, boy?" This time, Brody raised his head and with what looked like understanding in his eyes, responded with a loud bark as if he was in agreement with Cliff. "Besides," Cliff added, "tonight it's all about the book." He had waited long enough to be clued in on the mystery so he would have to keep his focus there instead of being in the presence of his beautiful red-headed date. "Come on boy let's get you some dinner so we can head out." With the thought of getting fed, Brody stood up, shook and with his tail wagging, followed his master into the kitchen.

Serena, now dressed in her new sweater that fit her form nicely and paired with her black leggings and boots, answered her shop door around 6:20. Cliff, looking sexy as usual in his Levis, boots and flannel was holding a half case of Blue Moon in one hand and the other was wrapped around a delicate bouquet of pink roses. If that wasn't enough Brody was also holding a thornless rose in his mouth. The site was enough to melt Serena's heart and almost brought tears to her eyes. It was a Kodak moment, she felt like the luckiest girl in the world. Capturing the moment she reached for her phone in her back pocket and snapped a picture of them. Afterward, Cliff handed the roses to Serena and kissed her softly on her luscious cherry glossed lips and headed towards the stairs. He put his free arm around her waist and marveled on how naturally beautiful she always seemed to look. Thinking to himself, he was one lucky man. He only hoped Serena was feeling the same way towards him.

The pizza was delivered shortly after Cliff arrived. They ate at her little kitchen table that was now adorned with her favorite vase filled with the pink roses. They sat across from each other caught up in their own thoughts, probably wondering what the night would bring. Looking at the handsome man staring across from her, Serena thought of how this seemed so comfortable to her and that she could get used to him being here. He even brought her pink roses, she swooned to herself. Pulling herself out of her little daydream, she was first to break the silence. "Thank you so much for the roses. How did you know they were my favorite or was it just a lucky guess?" Serena asked.

"Well, I would like to say I am physic and take the credit but I can't." Cliff admitted raising his eyebrows. "I have a confession to make, I wanted to make a good impression so I called your sister and she told me you loved pink roses."

Serena was taking a drink of beer and almost choked when she heard his confession, reaching for a napkin she questioned Cliff, "You called Tess?" I am surprised my phone isn't blowing up with her texts or calls. I know she is going to want to know all the details. So did you tell her why? Serena asked.

"Calm down, I am sure everything is fine. I just told her it was a thank you gift, and she probably didn't read much into it," Cliff answered hoping to relieve Serena's anxiousness.

"Let's see," Serena said, "roses plus very handsome man, hmmm. Nope, she's not going to read anything into it." Serena added with a laugh. "If I know my sister she has already written a book on all her assumptions and is going to want answers soon."

Cliff smiled and replied, "Handsome huh." Then with a laugh he continued. "Well if she has then I am sure she has included Tom in the story and we are both going to have questions to answer." Cliff knew he would need to talk to Tom soon and come clean with his friend. It would be better if he heard it from him instead of a gossip line. If Serena was right, which he had no doubt she was, his friend probably had an ear full from his beautiful wife.

Serena, smiling at Cliff as she cleared the table stated, "Well, you had better work on coming up with some answers and fast, don't you think?" She added with a giggle.

Cliff just laughed as he helped Serena clean up after dinner. Afterwards, they carried their beer into the living room and took comfort on the sofa. .

Serena sat contemplating how she wanted to open the conversation about James. However, she had a confession to make before she opened that can of worms. Turning to Cliff Serena stated nervously rubbing her sweaty palms together."I owe you an apology for my actions this morning. I behaved badly this morning and pulled away from you. I got scared and confused and needed some space." Serena took a deep breath and continued. "All morning I kept thinking about you and the night we shared and how happy you made me feel. I couldn't get my mind off you and I was having a hard time focusing on my work. Even though thinking about starting a new relationship scared me to death, my heart was telling me to give us a try. Ecstatic to tell you immediately, I made you a coffee, informed Lucy and headed over to the jewelry shop. On my way, I got so caught up in my own excitement and was embracing the gorgeous day that I let my guard down. Anyway, I found myself in the alley and noticed I was being followed, I tried to hurry my way through but I wasn't fast enough. The next thing I knew I had been pushed from behind causing me to lose my footing and drop your coffee. I lost the grip on my pepper spray I was holding onto in my pocket when I had to use my hands to balance myself to keep from falling. That's why I was in the alley where you found me." Serena took a deep breath before continuing.

"I hope that you can forgive my actions at your house this morning and take this crazy girl back and give her another chance. Because I think I am falling in love with you."

Cliff was not expecting this from Serena, funny her words didn't shock him and send him running. He was, however, a little surprised, he had been afraid that she had stepped back from him but instead she had moved two steps towards him. He reached for her hands and squeezing them lightly as he looked deep into her glistening eyes and replied, "No I won't take you back" Cliff said, and before he could finish his sentence, he watched a tear escape out of Serena's glistening eyes. Catching the tear with his finger he finished his sentence. "The reason I can't take you back is because I never let you go." He watched as the expression on Serena's sad face was replaced with a loving smile. "I knew you needed space and time to figure out things especially coming out of an unhappy relationship. To be totally honest I think I fell into love with you when you fell into my arms the night in front of your store. I didn't know it then but I do now."

Cliff then pulled Serena close to him, cuddled her face in his hands and their lips joined drinking in each other as they consummated their love with a long passionate kiss.

Serena thought she could stay right here kissing this man forever. She shivered as she felt his tongue dancing with hers. He removed the clip from her hair and tangled his hand through the sexy mess. He laid her back on the couch and excited greedy hands searched frantically for zippers and buttons. At that moment, nothing else mattered but their joining of bodies and falling into a blissful erotic ecstasy. Serena was suddenly brought back to present when she heard James yell out to her. **"Serena, please control yourself, I can sense you from in your bedroom the energy in here is overheating."**

As much as Serena wanted to get lost in this man she knew she needed to talk to Cliff about the book. Serena slowly pulled herself away from Cliff and whispered his name in his ear.

"Hmmm," Cliff mumbled, coming out of the sensual induced coma.

"I would love to stay here all night wrapped in your love but I really should tell you about the book," Serena replied.

"Oh, yes the book." Cliff replied as his focused returned. "I almost forgot about that, see what you do to me." He said with a laugh as he lifted himself off of Serena and tried to pull himself together.

Serena sat up and trying to make herself presentable, she fought with the hair clip to tame her wild hair. Then she reached for her chapstick and smiled as she applied a coat to her lips, still swollen from the kiss.

Standing and almost back to normal, Serena went to get the book out of her room. Serena picked up the book and whispered to James, "Sorry," she said out of courtesy, but if she had to be totally honest with herself, she wasn't sorry at all. But that would be rude and Serena was raised to mind her manners.

"No problem," James replied, then added, "I am glad that you two are finally together and as soon I can get free I will be out of your hair and let you live your life."

Serena felt a little sad when she thought about James not being here anymore. But what did she expect to keep him here forever. It wouldn't be fair to him and her life was complicated enough without trying to hide the mystery of a book from her family and friends.

"I can't really explain it Serena; I don't quite understand the physics of it myself. But when the two of you connect, the chemistry between you two causes a powerful surge of energy that locks into me somehow and drains my life source. Besides I feel like Peeping Tom," James admitted.

"Wow, I had no idea it affected you in that manner. I

promise I will be more cautious next time." Thinking to herself about what James shared with her, she realized there was so much she didn't know about his world, like energy forces and other strange things about the spirit realm. She wondered if there was a book on "The Spirit World for Dummies."

Serena stopped at the kitchen on her way back and calling to Cliff she asked, "Cliff you want me to bring you another beer?"

Cliff, who was relaxing in the living room as he waited for Serena, thought he had heard her talking to someone in her bedroom. Maybe his head wasn't as clear as he thought. Cliff knew another beer would only add to his confused mind so he opted for coffee instead. "I'm going to pass on the beer but I would take a coffee if it's not too much trouble."

"No trouble, but you sure you don't want a beer?" She asked again, trying to get him in a more relaxed state of mind. Maybe it would help to shield the shock.

"Coffee's fine." Cliff answered back.

"Coffee it is. It will just take me a couple minutes to make and then I will join you." Serena called back to Cliff. Softly whispering to James she commented with a nervous chuckle, "We will join you."

"Do you think he is going to believe us?" James asked.

"I don't know. It's hard to tell." Serena answered

pondering that thought as she prepared the coffee in the Keurig.

"Would you believe us, if you were in his shoes?" Serena asked trying to keep her voice low.

"I see your point," I'm sure it's all going to work out. He loves you and nothing should change that, even something this extreme," James replied

"I sure hope your right," Serena commented as she picked up the book and coffee.

"You ready for this," asked James.

"As ready as I'm going to get," Serena admitted who was trying to be positive as she carried the coffee and the spirit into the living room.

Cliff smiled and thanked Serena as she handed him his coffee. He was right he had heard her talking but her voice had been so soft and quiet he couldn't make out what was being said. He hoped he hadn't fallen in love with a schizophrenic. He was going to go with the assumption that she was talking to herself. That he could live with, the other; he had been there, done that and was never going through it again. Playing the detective; scoping out some answers he confronted Serena in a roundabout non-threatening way. "Funny I thought I heard you talking in the kitchen but it must've been the radio." He stated, curiously waiting for her reply.

"No radio," Serena answered taking a moment to pause before continuing. "I was talking to James, the spirit in the book. James meet Cliff and Cliff meet James," she said as she placed the book in his lap and stepped away waiting for his reaction.

Serena observed Cliff as he looked down at the book and back up at her with a puzzled look on his face. She wasn't totally surprised when he gave her the deer in the headlights look. She could imagine that in his mind, right now, he was probably questioning her sanity. The look, however, did terrify Serena to some degree and she was having second thoughts about telling him. What had she been thinking? He was never going to believe her. What if he thought she was crazy and decided to end their newly found relationship? Serena just couldn't face that possibility. Maybe she could laugh and say she was kidding and make up some more realistic story. She became lost and confused as she stood stuck in the moment as Cliff's skeptic eyes stared back at her.

"Cliff, please say something." Serena pleaded.

"Wow!" Cliff replied as he looked down at the book Serena had placed in his lap. He wondered if he had made a huge mistake getting involved with this redhead, who he was hoping wasn't crazy. He didn't want to believe that about Serena and thinking to himself, there must be a logical explanation for her odd behavior tonight.

Cliff after a heavy sigh voiced his opinion to Serena. "I am having a hard time wrapping my head around all this. I'd like to believe you but I am finding it difficult to even imagine what you said could be true. It goes way beyond my realm of possibilities. I think I need a little time to let it all soak in before we go any further with this discussion."

Cliff set the book on the table next to him, stood up, pulled Serena close to him and lifting up her chin staring into her eyes, he continued. "I know you said to keep an open mind and believe me I am trying. Who knows maybe things will look clearer after I have slept on it, which reminds me, I have an early morning appointment and it's after ten, so I should get going soon." Cliff brought his lips to hers and gave Serena a loving kiss and before saying goodbye he announced, "I will call you tomorrow, don't worry we'll work this out."

Serena was at a loss for words as she watched Cliff and Brody walk out the door. Struggling to pull in her emotions, Serena worked to stay positive as she gave James words of encouragement. "Well, that didn't go to terribly bad, not like we had planned but it could have been worse."

"What do you mean? Serena, if you haven't noticed, Cliff left before we had a chance to explain." James sarcastically replied.

"Yes I know that, but he also said we'd talk about it tomorrow. James, I was in denial when I first found out about you but in time, I came around. Cliff will too, you'll see. We just need to work on him a little more."

"I hope you're right," James answered with an uncertainty in his voice.

Me too, Serena thought to herself. Then with that, they said goodnight and Serena prepared for bed. Before falling asleep she thought about her life and where it was going. Even though it seemed crazy at times, especially since she was stuck in the middle of Cliff and James, she wouldn't trade it. They were two amazing souls, coming from completely different worlds, that had found their way into her heart and she could only hope they would find a way to connect to each other. Pondering that thought, she started to doze off but was suddenly awakened by a loud pounding sound coming from her front door.

WATCH FOR:

THE SPIRIT OF LOVE: LOST AND FOUND

THE NEXT BOOK IN THE "SPIRIT OF LOVE" SERIES
BY LINDA K. RICHISON

You won't want to miss the next episode, as the exciting and adventurous quest to free James continues. The chemistry between Serena and Cliff is sure to sizzle as they are pulled closer to one another while unraveling the clues. And on top of an already chaotic situation surrounding the book, new characters appear in Serena's life and they all seem to have their own unique twists to add, in solving the mystery.

ABOUT THE AUTHOR

Linda K. Richison lives with her loving husband and their three furry kids in Oregon. Her passions are singing, dancing and writing also spending time outdoors. She loves to get together with family and friends and values her time with her six precious grandchildren.

17790207R00149